Enid Blyton

STORIES OF

MAGIC
AND
MISCHIEF

Look out for all of these enchanting story collections

by *Enid Blyton*

SEASONAL COLLECTIONS

Springtime Stories
Holiday Stories
Summer Holiday Stories
Summertime Stories
Christmas Tales
Christmas Treats
Winter Stories

OTHER COLLECTIONS

Brer Rabbit
Cherry Tree Farm
Fireworks in Fairyland
Mr Galliano's Circus
Stories of Magic and Mischief
Stories of Wizards and Witches
The Wizard's Umbrella

Enid Blyton®
STORIES OF
MAGIC
AND
MISCHIEF

Hodder
Children's
Books

HODDER CHILDREN'S BOOKS

This collection first published in Great Britain in 2018
by Hodder & Stoughton

1 3 5 7 9 10 8 6 4 2

Enid Blyton® and Enid Blyton's signature are
registered trade marks of Hodder & Stoughton Limited
Text © 2018 Hodder & Stoughton Limited
Illustrations © 2018 Hodder & Stoughton Limited

A CIP catalogue record for this book is available from the British Library.

ISBN 978 1 444 94257 6

Printed and bound in Great Britain by Clays Ltd, Elcograf S.p.A

The paper and board used in this book are made from wood from
responsible sources.

Hodder Children's Books
An imprint of Hachette Children's Group
Part of Hodder & Stoughton
Carmelite House
50 Victoria Embankment
London EC4Y 0DZ

An Hachette UK Company
www.hachette.co.uk
www.hachettechildrens.co.uk

Contents

The Goblin's Dog

The Goblin's Dog

ONCE UPON a time there lived a little boy called Willie. He had a dog named Tinker, and they often went for walks together.

Tinker was fond of Willie, but the little boy was not very kind to his dog. He was supposed to look after him and care for him, but many a time he went off to play and forgot all about him.

Tinker lived in a kennel out in the yard. It was a nice kennel, but it needed new straw each day. Sometimes Willie remembered, and sometimes he didn't.

Tinker liked fresh water to drink, but often Willie forgot all about refilling his water bowl. And once poor Tinker had no water at all because someone had upset it, and Willie hadn't noticed.

'Willie, it's cold weather now,' his mother said to him one day. 'Have you seen that Tinker has plenty of good warm straw in his kennel?'

'Yes, Mother,' said Willie. But, you know, he hadn't – and Tinker had made his old straw so flat that there was no warmth in it at all. So he was cold at night when the frosts came. He thought of Willie in his warm bed, and how he longed to be able to curl up there with him. But he had to stay in his icy-cold kennel.

Now, one night a small brownie came by on the way to the dairy to get a drink of milk. He heard Tinker shivering and popped his head into the kennel.

'What's the matter with you?' he said. 'You seem very cold! Haven't you any warm straw?'

'Not much,' said Tinker. 'And my water is frozen too, so that I can't get a drink if I want to. Willie didn't take me for a run either, so I haven't been able to get warm. Do you think you could bring me some water, brownie? There is some in the stream not far away.'

'Certainly,' said the brownie. He broke the ice in the bowl, emptied it out and ran to the stream. He came back with some water and put it beside the kennel. 'I wish I could get you some straw too,' he said. 'But I don't know where there is any.'

'Never mind,' said Tinker gratefully. 'Perhaps Willie will remember to get some tomorrow.'

The brownie went to the dairy and had a drink of milk. He was unhappy because he couldn't forget the poor cold dog. He wished he could get some straw. He remembered that a wizard lived not far off, and he thought that maybe he would know how to make straw out of magic. So he went to his house and knocked.

A black cat opened the door and the brownie went in. Soon he had told the wizard all about Tinker. The wizard listened and he frowned deeply.

'That boy should be taught a lesson,' he said. He clapped his hands and the black cat appeared.

'Fetch the policeman,' said the wizard. The cat disappeared, and when it came back, it brought with it a large policeman with pink wings and a shiny face.

'Go and arrest Willie, who lives at the farmhouse,' commanded the wizard. 'Bring him before the court tomorrow, charged with neglecting his dog.'

The policeman saluted, flapped his pink wings and disappeared.

And soon, what a shock poor Willie got! He was sound asleep when he awoke to find a lantern shining on his face. The shiny-faced policeman was standing nearby, and he spoke sternly to Willie.

'Come with me, little boy. I arrest you for neglecting your dog!'

Willie put on his coat and went with the policeman. The big policeman suddenly spread his wings and flew through the night, carrying Willie firmly in his arms. There was no escape at all!

The little boy spent the night at the wizard's, and then the next morning the policeman took him to a big courthouse. Inside there was a judge who sat solemnly at a high bench, and had great wings like a butterfly's wings behind him. There were twelve pixies, brownies and gnomes sitting at a table below, and there were six policemen, all with pink wings.

'This is Willie,' said the policeman who had fetched the little boy. 'He is here because of the following things: forgetting to give his dog fresh water, forgetting to give him straw for his kennel, forgetting to take him for a run and altogether being very unkind.'

'Very bad,' said the judge, frowning at Willie. 'Very bad indeed! Jurymen, what punishment shall we have?'

The twelve pixies, brownies and gnomes who sat below the judge began to talk excitedly among themselves. Then a long-bearded gnome stood up.

'If you please, your worship,' he said to the judge.

'We think he should be turned into a dog and sent to one of the goblins.'

'Certainly, certainly,' said the judge. 'A very good idea!'

'But you can't do that!' cried poor Willie. 'Why, my mother would wonder where I am!'

'Well, we will make your dog Tinker change into you,' said the judge. 'It will be a treat for him to have good food, plenty of fresh water to drink and a warm bed at night. Now stand still please, Willie!'

Willie stood still, wondering what was going to happen. The judge took up a wand that lay beside him, leant over to Willie and tapped him on the shoulder, saying, 'A curious punishment you'll see! A boy you are – a dog you'll be!'

And then he said a very magic word – and my goodness me, Willie found that black hair was growing all over his body! His clothes disappeared. He grew a long tail. His ears became furry. His nose became long and he had paws instead of his hands and feet. He was a little black dog, and when he opened his mouth to speak he could only say, 'Woof, woof, woof!'

'Take him to the goblin Workalot,' commanded the judge. So Willie was led out of the court on a chain and taken to a small cottage in a wood. Here a little green goblin lived. He didn't seem at all pleased to see Willie.

'I don't really want a dog,' he said to the policeman who brought Willie. 'Dogs are a nuisance. But if the judge says I'm to have him, I suppose I must.'

There was no kennel for Willie so he hoped he would sleep on a nice warm rug in front of the kitchen fire. But a big grey cat suddenly appeared as soon as Willie sat down on the rug.

'*Phizzz-ss-ss-ss!*' she hissed at poor Willie. He ran back in fright, and got between the legs of the goblin who was just coming in with a bowl of water. Down went the goblin, and all the water splashed over Willie.

'Clumsy creature!' cried Workalot. He gave Willie

a cuff on the head. Willie hoped he would get a towel and dry him, but he didn't. So the dog sat in a corner and shivered, for he did not dare to go near the fire when the cat was there.

Workalot was a very busy goblin. He ran here and there, he did this and that, and he grumbled and talked to himself all the time. The grey cat did nothing, but when Workalot needed help with a spell, she walked up and sat solemnly in the middle of a big chalk circle.

Soon Willie began to feel very hungry indeed. The cat had a good dinner of fish and milk put down for her, but the goblin did not give Willie any dinner.

'I'll give you something later on!' he grumbled. But he quite forgot, so poor Willie had to go without. He thought he would whine so that Workalot would take notice of him. But as soon as he began yelping and whining, the goblin lost his temper. Willie put his tail down and ran under the table. But the goblin pulled him out, took him to the door and put him outside.

It was pouring with rain. Willie looked around for

shelter, but there was only one bush growing in the garden. He ran to that and crouched underneath, cold, wet and hungry. How dreadful it was to be a dog owned by an unkind master with no love in him!

The rain stopped. Willie crept out from the bush, but the door was shut and he could not get into the house. He looked at the house next door. A dog lived there too. But it was a dog that somebody loved, for it was well-brushed, cheerful and not at all thin. Willie wished he belonged to a good home too. How lovely it would be to be petted and well looked after!

The door opened and the goblin whistled. Willie ran in. The cat spat at him and Willie growled back. Workalot gave him a cuff. 'Leave my cat alone!' he said. 'Go into the corner and lie down.'

Willie lay down. The cat sat in front of the warm fire and washed herself. There was an empty bowl not far from her, and Willie felt sure that it had been put down for him – with some meat and biscuits in, perhaps – and the cat had eaten it all up.

Willie fell asleep at last. But when night came, the goblin woke him up by fastening a chain to his collar and dragging him outside. He had put an old barrel there, on its side, and in the barrel he had put a handful of straw. 'Get in!' said the goblin. 'And mind you bark if the enemy comes!'

Poor Willie! He didn't know who the enemy was – and he was very frightened to think they might come! He was cold too, for the wind blew right into his barrel, and he was so thirsty that he would have been glad to lick the snow, if there had been any. He began to whine dismally.

Out flew the goblin in a fine rage and shouted at him.

After that, Willie didn't dare to make another sound. He just lay silent and hoped that the enemy wouldn't come.

Suddenly, at midnight, he heard a little scraping sound at the gate and he stiffened in fear. The enemy! The gate swung open and in came . . . whoever do you think? Why, nobody else but Tinker the dog! He ran up to Willie's barrel and sniffed at him.

'I heard you were here, changed into a dog,' he said. 'They changed me into you – but I changed back at midnight and I've come to rescue you. You were never very kind to me, Willie, but I love you and would do anything for you. Now keep still and I'll gnaw right through your collar.'

Willie was full of gratitude to the little dog. He kept still, and very soon Tinker's sharp teeth had bitten right through the leather. He was free!

'Come on!' whispered Tinker. 'I know the way.'

The two dogs sped through the night and at last came to the farmhouse. 'Go to your room and get into your bed,' said Tinker. 'In the morning you will be yourself.'

Willie pushed his way into the house and ran up the stairs. He jumped into his warm bed and was soon asleep. In the morning he was himself again.

It's all very strange, thought Willie as he dressed.

How kind Tinker was! How awful it is to be a dog belonging to an unkind master. I have been unkind to Tinker often. I never will be again!

He ran down into the yard. Tinker was in his kennel. He wagged his tail. 'Tinker! Tinker!' said Willie, putting his arms round the little dog. 'Thank you for rescuing me! I'm sorry I was unkind to you. I will always love you now, and look after you properly!'

And so he did. Tinker has a warm kennel, plenty of fresh water each day, good food, a fine walk in the morning and lots of pats. He is very happy – and I do hope your dog is too!

The Most Peculiar Knocker

The Most Peculiar
Knocker

IN HURRY-UP Village there lived some naughty goblin children called Tuffy, Smick and Woff. The tricks they got up to!

They would lean over the walls of people's back gardens and snip their clothes lines so that the clothes would tumble right down into the mud.

They would all climb up to the little bedroom that Tuffy had at the top of his house, and pour water down on passers-by. And then they would go up to people's front doors and knock loudly and run away.

So you can see that they were really a perfect nuisance. 'There go Tuffy, Smick and Woff,' the people would say, seeing the three children going down the street. 'I wonder what mischief they're up to now?'

One day Mr Candleshoe came to live in the cottage at the end of the street. He was a funny old fellow, who always sang little songs to himself whenever he went out. Tuffy and the others thought it would be fine fun to tease him.

'He's got a wonderful new knocker on his door,' said Tuffy. 'It's a really strange one – just like a man's hand! I guess it must have been a magic one at some time or other.'

It certainly was a peculiar knocker. It knocked extremely loudly too, but that was a good thing because Mr Candleshoe was rather deaf, and he wouldn't have heard if anyone had knocked softly.

Ratta-tatta-TAT! said the knocker loudly, when the postman called.

Ratta-TATTA-TAT! it said even more loudly, when Mr Candleshoe's friend Mr Sharp-Eye called.

Mr Sharp-Eye was a wizard, it was said. He knew a lot of spells, and Tuffy, Woff and Smick kept out of his way. They didn't like the way he looked at them when they met him!

'I feel he might turn me into a black beetle or something,' said Smick, 'and I don't like it.'

Now, Tuffy soon found that it was fun to bang Mr Candleshoe's knocker. The first time he did it, he had to deliver a parcel there. He crashed the knocker up and down.

RATTA-TATTA-RATTA-TATTA! The noise almost made Mr Candleshoe jump out of his skin.

'Jumping pigs and piglets!' he cried. 'What's that?'

He hurried to the door, falling over the mat on the way. Tuffy thought it really was one of the funniest things he had ever seen.

'Now don't you crash on my door like that again,' said Mr Candleshoe, when he saw Tuffy. 'I won't have it! You're a bad goblin. I shan't give you any money for bringing the parcel.'

Ho! thought Tuffy, going down the steps. *Oho! So he won't give me any money, the mean old miser! Well I'll soon make him wish he had!*

He went to find Smick and Woff. He told them how he had crashed the knocker on Mr Candleshoe's door and made the old man jump. 'He's a mean fellow,' said Tuffy. 'We'll go and do a lot more crashing, shall we?'

So Smick used to go and knock loudly on his way to school in the morning, and Woff used to do it whenever he passed, which was quite often.

Ratta-tatta-TAT! RATTA-TAT! You should have heard that knocker going – morning, afternoon and evening! Mr Candleshoe would jump out of his chair and tear to the door – and nobody would be there!

He was puzzled at first. He thought whoever was there must be invisible. But they weren't, of course. They had just run away.

Then Mr Candleshoe gave up going to the door to open it. But the very times he didn't go, it would be the postman with a parcel, or Mrs Lucy coming along with a dish of hot cakes, or the milkman asking if he wanted any cream left that day.

'What am I to do, what am I to do?' said poor old Mr Candleshoe to his friend, Mr Sharp-Eye. 'That knocker makes me jump from morning to night – and when I answer the door, there's nobody there – and if I don't answer it there's sure to be somebody!'

'You want a little magic rubbed into the knocker!' said Mr Sharp-Eye with a grin. 'That's what you want, my good friend. I'll put some there for you. Let's see – your knocker is in the shape of a big hand, isn't it? I'll just go and rub a little of my yellow ointment into it. You'll soon find out who comes and bangs on it, Mr Candleshoe. And your knocker will hold him tight for you!'

Mr Sharp-Eye rubbed in the magic ointment. Then he said goodbye to Mr Candleshoe and went home.

It wasn't long before Tuffy was along that way again. He looked up the street and down. Nobody about. Now for a good old crash with that knocker! He'd make Mr Candleshoe fall out of his chair with fright!

But it so happened that Mr Candleshoe had gone out just after his friend had walked home, and there was nobody in his cottage! So when Tuffy rapped on the knocker, RATTA-TATTA-TAT, there was no one indoors to hear it.

Tuffy had tight hold of the knocker as he knocked – but something strange happened before he had finished. The brass knocker, which was shaped like a hand, suddenly took hold of him! Yes, it twisted round and held Tuffy's hand so tightly that he squealed!

'Oooh! What's happening? Ooh! Let go, let go! Ooooh!'

Tuffy couldn't take his hand away! The knocker had got it far too tightly. He pulled and he tugged, but it wasn't a bit of good. He couldn't get away.

Then he guessed what had happened. Mr

22

Candleshoe had some magic in his knocker, and the knocker was busy using it! It would hold Tuffy there till Mr Candleshoe came back – and then what would happen?

Tuffy began to squeal. His two friends Smick and Woff came by and they stopped when they heard Tuffy's yells. 'What's the matter?' they shouted in surprise.

'Come and pull, come and pull!' cried Tuffy. 'This knocker's got hold of me!'

So Smick and Woff went to pull and, dear me, they pulled so hard that the knocker came right off the door! Then Tuffy raced home as fast as he could, afraid that Mr Candleshoe might come back and catch him if he stayed a moment longer.

The knocker still had hold of his hand! Tuffy couldn't get rid of it. It held tightly on to his fingers and it wouldn't let them go at all!

Tuffy put it into ice-cold water. No good. Then he put it into very hot water and almost scalded the skin off his own hand. No good at all! The knocker held him as tightly as ever.

Then Tuffy knew that nothing would ever make the magic knocker let go of his hand, unless Mr Candleshoe helped, and he began to howl.

In came his father and mother, alarmed. When they saw Tuffy and the knocker, they were even more astonished.

'Get it off, oh, please get it off!' wept Tuffy.

'It's a knocker!' said his father. 'And it looks like Candleshoe's too. Tuffy, how did you come to get it like this?'

Tuffy wailed out his story. His father listened sternly. 'Ah – at last you have found someone who can punish you for playing your silly, annoying tricks!' he said. 'Well, Tuffy, either you will have to live with that knocker, or you will have to go to Mr Candleshoe and confess to him what has happened!'

'I'm afraid to do that, I'm afraid!' howled Tuffy.

But he had to go in the end because, you see, he

couldn't write, or wash his hand properly, or even undress, with the knocker holding him by the hand like that!

'Ha!' said Mr Candleshoe, when Tuffy stood before him, his face red with crying. 'So it was you trying to be funny, bringing me to the door a dozen times a day! Well, I think that you've got a fine punishment!'

'Please take the knocker off my hand!' wept Tuffy. 'Please take it off.'

'I've got a new knocker now,' said Mr Candleshoe. 'I don't need that one. You can have it.'

'I don't *wannnt* it!' wailed Tuffy. 'Oh, take it off, Mr Candleshoe, and I'll never never be bad again.'

'Well – I'll take it off,' said Mr Candleshoe, 'but I don't want it back. It can live with you, Tuffy. But I warn you – if you get up to any tricks, the knocker will chase you and try to take hold of your hand once more!'

And goodness me, it does! His father never needs

to punish Tuffy now. Whenever he's naughty, the knocker jumps up from its corner and chases him round the room. What a fine time that knocker has and no mistake! I'm sure Tuffy's sorry now that he ever played the silly game of knocking at doors and running away.

The Bonfire Folk

The Bonfire Folk

PETER AND JEAN were running home from school one day when they passed the cobbler's shop. Mr Knock the cobbler was sitting cross-legged in his window, mending somebody's shoes.

His glass window was closed, for it was a cold day. Peter knocked on it, for he and Jean always liked to have a smile from the old cobbler. He had eyes as blue as forget-me-nots and whiskers as white as snow.

Mr Knock looked up and smiled, then beckoned the children inside. They opened the door and walked in, sniffing the good smell of leather.

'Did you want us, Mr Knock?' asked Peter.

'Yes,' said Mr Knock. 'I want to know if you'll do an old man a good turn. My boy's ill and there are three pairs of shoes to be sent out. Do you think you and Jean could deliver them for me on your way home?'

'Of course, Mr Knock,' said Peter. 'We'd love to. Where are they?'

The old cobbler gave three parcels to them. 'That's for Captain Brown,' he said. 'That's for Mrs Lee – and that little one is for Mrs George's baby. You know where they all live, don't you?'

'Yes, Mr Knock!' said the children, pleased. It was fun to play at being errand boys! They rushed off with the parcels and left them at the right houses. Then they went home to dinner. On their way to afternoon school they went to see Mr Knock again.

'We delivered all your parcels safely for you,' said Peter.

'Thank you kindly,' said Mr Knock. 'Now what would you like for a reward?'

'Nothing!' said Jean at once. 'We did it for you

because we like you. We don't want to be paid.'

'Well, I won't pay you,' said Mr Knock, his blue eyes shining. 'But I happen to know something you badly want and maybe I'll be able to help you to get it. I know that you want to see the fairy folk, don't you?'

'Oooh, yes,' said both children at once, 'but we never have.'

'Well, I'll tell you a time *I* saw them,' said Mr Knock, almost in a whisper. 'I saw them one cold December night, my dears – all toasting themselves beside my father's bonfire at the bottom of the garden. I've never told anyone till today – but now I'm telling you, for maybe you'll see them there too!'

Well! The children were so surprised that they could hardly say a word. They went off to school full of excitement. Daddy was at home that day and meant to make a bonfire, they knew. Suppose, just suppose they saw the little folk round the flames?

They went down to look at the bonfire after school. Daddy said he was going to let it out soon and the children were disappointed. They ran off to some woods nearby and, in the half-dark, managed to find some dry fir cones. 'We'll use these to keep the fire going after tea,' said Jean. 'They burn beautifully.'

They placed a little pile of them beside the still-burning fire and ran in to tea – but afterwards Auntie Millie came and the two children had to stay and talk to her. It was their bedtime before they could think of going down to the bonfire again.

'Let's creep down now and see if anyone is there,' said Jean. 'I *would* so like to see. It's very cold and frosty tonight – maybe there will be one or two of the little folk there already.'

They put on their coats, their hats and their scarves. They opened the garden door softly. They crept down the garden, walking on the grass so that their feet should make no noise.

'The bonfire is still burning,' whispered Jean. 'It didn't go out after all. Can you see anyone there?'

The children went round a hedge and came in sight

of the fire. It was burning brightly and the smoke swirled away from it, smelling delicious. Jean and Peter stopped and looked.

'There's Whiskers, our cat, sitting by it!' said Jean in a delighted whisper. 'And look – there's the cat next door too! Both warming their toes!'

'What's that the other side?' whispered back Peter. 'I think – I really do think it's a brownie!'

It was! He was a tiny little man with a long beard and twinkling eyes. He was throwing fir cones on the fire. No wonder it was burning brightly!

'It's the fir cones we collected!' said Jean. 'How lovely! Oh, look – here's someone coming!'

Somebody came out of the shadowy bushes and sat down by the fire. It was an elf with long shining wings. She spoke to the cats and the brownie and they all nodded to her. They knew one another, it was quite certain. The fairy had brought some bundles of small twigs with her and these she threw every now and again on the fire, making it burn even more brightly.

Then a hedgehog came – and a rabbit. They sat down by the bonfire, and the rabbit held out both his paws to the flames. Jean and Peter thought he looked lovely.

'Isn't this exciting?' whispered Jean. 'I never thought we'd see all this! Do you suppose everybody's bonfires have bonfire folk round them at night?'

'I expect so,' said Peter. 'Oh, Jean – do let's go and speak to them all! I'm sure they won't be frightened.'

The two children left the hedge they were standing by and walked softly to the bonfire. Nobody saw them at first – and then the two cats pricked up their ears, spied them both and shot away like shadows.

Peter caught hold of the brownie and held him tightly. 'Don't be afraid,' he said. 'I just want to speak to you. This is our bonfire and we are so pleased to see you come and warm yourselves by it. I am glad you used the fir cones to make it burn brightly.'

'Oh, did *you* leave the fir cones?' said the brownie. 'How kind of you! The fire was nearly out, but the dry cones just got it going again nicely. You're sure you don't mind us warming ourselves here? It's so very cold tonight – and these garden bonfires are so useful to us little folk.'

'You come whenever you like,' said Peter, letting go the brownie now that the little man knew the children were friends. For a few minutes they all sat there together, and the rabbit was just about to jump on to Jean's knee when the children heard their mother calling.

'Peter! Jean! You naughty children! Surely you haven't gone out into the cold garden! Come to bed at once.'

'Goodbye!' said the children to the bonfire folk. 'Tell everybody to use our fire each night. We like to know you are there.' And off they ran to bed.

They love to think of all the little bonfire folk sitting round the smoky fire in the garden. Do *you* ever have a bonfire? Well, maybe the little folk are round yours too, warming their toes on a winter's evening! Wouldn't I love to see them!

Tell-Tale!

Tell-Tale!

'HERE COMES Tell-Tale!' said Jinks. 'Hallo Tell-Tale! That tongue of yours is ready to say something nasty, I'm sure!'

'My name is Roundy, not Tell-Tale,' said the little goblin crossly. 'I'm always telling you that.'

'And we're always forgetting,' said Gobo. 'And we shall go on forgetting till you stop telling tales!'

'I don't tell tales,' said Tell-Tale. 'I just spread the news. I say – have you heard about Mr Stamp-About? He has quarrelled with his old aunt and he called her Mrs Stick-in-the-Mud. I heard him.'

'Tell-tale!' said Jinks at once.

The little goblin ran off angrily and looked about for Mrs Listen-Hard. She loved to hear his tales. He met her just down the street. 'Oh, Mrs Listen-Hard,' he said. 'Have you heard the latest about the baker's bread? Well, somebody found a mouse tail in a loaf! What do you think of that?'

'Shocking!' said Mrs Listen-Hard. 'Whatever next will he put into his loaves?'

'And did you hear that Jinny Jinks was rude to her teacher yesterday and had to stand in the corner all the morning?' said Tell-Tale. 'All the Jinks children are cheeky – I'd like to stand each of them in a corner. The way they call out after me when I go by!'

'Dear, dear!' said Mrs Listen-Hard. 'Well, some people do bring up their children badly, I'm sure!'

Tell-Tale ran around all day long telling his nasty little tales.

He never said anything nice about anyone, but, as tell-tales do, he picked up all the unpleasant bits of news that he could find, and passed them on.

Nobody could stop him; Jinks wouldn't speak to him for a whole month, but Tell-Tale didn't mind. He just went around saying that Jinks was so afraid of him that he dare not open his mouth when he, Tell-Tale, came by. That made Jinks cross and he gave Tell-Tale a stern scolding when he saw him next.

But even that didn't stop him. And then there came a day when he told tales to quite the wrong person!

It happened that the Wizard of Ho was coming to stay with his brother, Mr Kindly, in Tell-Tale's village. Tell-Tale got the news first and ran round to everyone.

'Have you heard the news about Mr Kindly's brother?' he asked. 'It's that horrible Wizard of Ho, you know. He's coming here to stay.'

'He's not horrible,' said Gobo. 'He's stern and very clever – but he's kind too, like his brother.'

'Well, I've heard tales about him that prove he's

not a bit kind,' said Tell-Tale. 'Did you know he once turned a dog into a shopping basket, just because it barked at him, and he goes shopping with that basket every day?'

'Rubbish!' said Gobo. 'Where do you pick up these extraordinary tales? You must make half of them up!'

'And did you hear that the wizard wouldn't...' began Tell-Tale again – but Gobo walked off. Tell-Tale stared after him angrily.

'How rude he is! I'll go and find Mrs Listen-Hard and tell her of Gobo's bad behaviour!'

Now, the next week, it happened that Tell-Tale had to walk to the farm to get some butter. On the way back he overtook a small cart, drawn by a donkey. It was driven by a funny old fellow, who sat on top of a pile of boxes and bags. He had on an old green suit, and wore a rather shabby hat with a green feather in it.

He called to Tell-Tale. 'Hey, you! Am I right for Apple-Tree Village?'

'Oh, no – you're on the wrong road,' said Tell-Tale. 'I'm on my way there, so I'll guide you if you like. It's my own village, so I know the way well.'

'Jump up then,' said the old fellow, and Tell-Tale leapt up and sat on a box.

'What's Apple-Tree Village like?' asked the old man, clicking to his donkey. 'It's a nice little place, I've heard, with kindly people.'

'Ah – that's what you've heard,' said Tell-Tale. 'The people are a strange lot – rude, you know – no manners. Some of them aren't honest either – or kind.'

'Dear, dear!' said the old fellow. 'But what about Dame Gentle and Mr Kindly? Surely they are like their names?'

'Not a bit!' said Tell-Tale, enjoying himself. 'Dame Gentle smacked me the other day – that shows how gentle she is! And as for Mr Kindly, nobody really likes him. He only pretends to be kind. And that reminds me, he's got a dreadful brother coming to stay with him – a horrible fellow called the Wizard of Ho.'

'Really?' said the old man. 'And what's so horrible about the Wizard of Ho?'

'Oh, haven't you heard?' said Tell-Tale. 'Well, it's said that he's not honest – he goes around stealing things he wants for his spells, if he can't buy them. He stole a bunch of peacock feathers out of Mrs Hey-Diddle's vase on her mantelpiece, when he went calling one day.'

'You don't say so!' said the old man.

'Yes – and he was once turned out of the palace for being rude to the prince himself,' said Tell-Tale. 'And he turned a dog into a shopping basket for barking at him. Oh, I tell you, he's a bad fellow, and nobody wants him to come and stay in the village.'

'Dear me!' said the old man.

'I can tell you, I shall say a few things to him that he won't like, if I see him,' said Tell-Tale. 'Nobody else will – they're too feeble for words in our village! I'm the only one that sticks up for my own ideas. I'll send that old wizard packing if he doesn't behave himself.'

'Is this the village?' said the old man, as they came to a row of pretty little houses.

'Yes,' said Tell-Tale. 'There's Mr Kindly's cottage, look. He's in his garden – looking out for someone, I should think.'

'Yes – he's looking out for me, I expect,' said the old man. 'He's my brother. I'm the Wizard of Ho. You've been telling me a lot of tales about myself – most interesting! I had never heard them before.'

Tell-Tale stared at him in horror. What – this funny old man was the great Wizard of Ho? Without his cloak, without his great pointed hat – no wonder he hadn't known him!

'Thank you for guiding me,' said the wizard, getting down. 'Here's something for your trouble.' He reached his hand up into the air – and brought down a parrot! A little parrot, straight out of the air. How extraordinary!

'It can talk like you,' said the wizard. 'It can tell tales, sometimes true, sometimes not, just like yours. It's exactly the right companion for you.'

The parrot flew straight on to Tell-Tale's shoulder and squawked in his ear, making him jump. 'You haven't washed behind your ears this morning!' it said. 'Dirty goblin.'

The wizard took no more notice of Tell-Tale but went to greet his brother, Mr Kindly. Tell-Tale fled down the street, very scared. Goodness – he might have been turned into a black beetle or a caterpillar! He ran into his house and slammed the door.

'Don't be noisy,' said the parrot on his shoulder. 'My word, what an untidy place! Don't you ever sweep the floor?'

'Look here – I'm not having this kind of talk from a parrot!' said Tell-Tale furiously, and tried to grab it off his shoulder. He got such a jab from its curved beak that he burst out crying.

'Well, what a crybaby!' said the parrot in a shocked voice. 'Where's your hanky? My, what a dirty one!'

There came a knock at the door, and the milkman put his head in. 'Any milk?' he said.

'Oh, milkman, yes – one pint,' said Tell-Tale. 'I say – did you hear that the baker put a mouse tail in one of his loaves?'

The parrot gave a squawk. 'Milkman, did you know that Tell-Tale doesn't sweep his floor? And I say, have you ever sat on his shoulder and looked behind his ears? He doesn't wash properly! And he's an awful crybaby. Just now—'

'*Will* you stop it!' cried Tell-Tale, in a rage. 'What do you mean saying all those things about me? I won't have it!'

The parrot nibbled his ear, and Tell-Tale yelled and tried to push him off. 'No use,' said the parrot.

'The wizard gave me to you, and here I stay. I'm a chatterbox, I am – just like you!'

What a truly dreadful time Tell-Tale had the next few days. He simply could not get rid of that parrot. It clung to his shoulder wherever he went – and it said the most dreadful things!

As soon as Tell-Tale told a tale about anyone, the parrot at once told a few about the goblin. 'Listen to me, listen to me!' it would squawk. 'Have you heard that Tell-Tale picks apples out of Dame Flap's garden at night? And did you know that he borrowed Flip's barrow and never took it back? It's in his shed. Squaawk!'

'Oh, you fibber!' cried Tell-Tale.

'Who's a fibber?' said the parrot, raising the feathers on its head angrily. 'You are! Who said the Wizard of Ho turned a dog into a shopping basket? You did. You're a fibber!'

'Will you be quiet?' shouted Tell-Tale.

'No,' said the parrot. 'I'm fond of talking, like

you. I'm fond of spreading tales. You can't blame me for that! You're fond of it too. Oh, I say, do you remember the time when you took the sweets away from Mother Jolly's little girl? And shall I tell you about the time when—'

Tell-Tale had to run back home and slam his door then. He just never knew what the parrot would say next. But he couldn't get rid of it. It sat on his shoulder day and night, and he dared not try to push it off because it pecked him so hard with its curved beak.

'You deafen me with your squawks!' complained Tell-Tale. 'I hate you! And how dare you tell all those wicked stories about me? They're not true!'

'Half of them are,' said the parrot, jigging up and down on Tell-Tale's shoulder in a most aggravating manner. 'Some of them aren't. But lots of the tales you tell aren't true either. You stop telling untruths and I will. See?'

'All right,' said Tell-Tale, who was really getting

most alarmed at the stories the parrot told about him. Why, if they came to the ears of the village policeman, he might quite well believe them and pop Tell-Tale into prison!

So Tell-Tale was very careful after that. He didn't tell any untrue tales – but he told plenty of true ones that were not very nice!

'Did you know that Mr and Mrs Binks had a dreadful quarrel yesterday?' he said. 'Did you hear that little Pinkity had to write out a hundred lines after school this morning – "I must not be rude to teacher." Did you know that—'

'My turn, my turn!' shouted the parrot. 'Did you know that Tell-Tale hasn't got a toothbrush, so he never cleans his teeth? Did you hear that he wouldn't pay old Mrs Needle what she asked him for making his new suit? Did you know that he never makes his bed, the dirty fellow? Did you—'

Tell-Tale was always going red in the face, always feeling ashamed, always running back home to stop the parrot saying any more. How he hated that bird! But he couldn't get rid of it, no matter what he did.

So one day he went to Mr Kindly's cottage, and asked to see the wizard. Mr Kindly took him into his little front room, where the wizard was reading a book on spells. Tell-Tale knelt down humbly.

'I have come to beg your pardon,' he said. 'Forgive me for all I said. And I do beg of you to take this parrot away – he is making my life miserable.'

'He is only doing what you have often done,' said the wizard. 'You have made many lives miserable with your tales. Why shouldn't you be made miserable too?'

'I'll never make people miserable again,' said Tell-Tale. 'Please take this hateful bird away.'

'Sir Wizard, did you know that Tell-Tale always...' began the bird. Tell-Tale began to cry.

'There you are, you see – he tells tales about me all the time. Take him away!'

'I can't,' said the wizard gravely. 'He'll be with you

always now. I made him out of your own nature, you know. He's part of you now. He'll never go away! You're a tell-tale fellow, and he's a tell-tale bird!'

Mr Kindly was sorry for poor Tell-Tale. He patted him on the shoulder. 'There's quite an easy way out,' he said. 'Turn over a new leaf, Tell-Tale. Make yourself kind and truthful – don't run about telling tales and making mischief – and this bird will copy you and be the same!'

'It isn't an easy way out!' wept Tell-Tale. 'It's the hardest thing in the world to change myself – you know that.'

The little goblin went off, and the tell-tale parrot screeched in delight. 'Did you know he went and fell on his knees before the Wizard of Ho? Did you hear that?'

Well – that was a whole year ago now and I expect you'd like to know what happened. Somebody went to Apple-Tree Village the other day and wanted to know where Tell-Tale lived.

'Tell-Tale? Who's he?' said Gobo. 'Oh, you mean Roundy – the nice little fellow who's got a talking parrot? We don't call him Tell-Tale any more you know. Everyone likes him now – and as for the parrot, well it's a real pet!'

So now we know what happened! Good for you, Tell-Tale – oh, no – I mean, Roundy!

A Peculiar Adventure

A Peculiar Adventure

'MIAOW!' SAID a voice, just down by Ronnie's feet. He looked down, but he couldn't see anything, which wasn't very surprising because there was a thick fog that hid even the houses nearby.

'Where are you?' said Ronnie. 'You're a cat, I suppose, and you're lost in the fog.'

'MIAOW!' said the cat in a louder voice, and rubbed itself against Ronnie's legs. He switched on his torch and looked down.

'My word! What a wonderful cat you are!' he said. 'As black as soot and with eyes as green as cucumbers. Are you lost? Where do you live?'

'*Miaow-ee-ow-ee-ow,*' said the cat, as if it was explaining where its home was. Then Ronnie noticed that it wore a little collar round its neck with a disc hanging from it. Perhaps its name and address were on that. He looked at the disc in the light of his torch.

'Yes – here's your name, I suppose – Cinders – and your address – Wizard Cottage, Hanger Lane. Well, Hanger Lane isn't far away, Cinders, so I'll take you there and find your house. Wizard Cottage! What a strange name for a house. I've never noticed it before. Come along. Keep at my heels and we'll soon be there.'

The cat kept close to Ronnie as he went down the road and round the corner. The little boy flashed his torch on the name on each gate.

'Holly Trees. That's not it. Little Abbey. That's not it either. What's this one? Red Roofs. I do hope we shan't have to go all down the road before we find it, and then back again down the opposite side!'

'Miaow!' said the cat. Ronnie went on down the road, looking for Wizard Cottage – and there it was, the very, very last house in the row, the one on the corner. Its name was on the gate: Wizard Cottage.

'Here we are,' said Ronnie. 'Shall I ring the bell and hand you in, puss? If I leave you wandering about outside you may get lost again. I'll ring or knock.'

He knocked, because there was no bell. The knocker was very strange. It was in the shape of a hand, and Ronnie felt as if it was shaking hands with him when he knocked.

The door opened, but nobody stood behind it. Ronnie hesitated. He didn't like to go in. But the cat walked straight in, turned round and looked at Ronnie.

'Miaow!' it said politely.

'DO COME IN!' shouted a voice. 'And shut the door. The fog's spoiling my work.'

Ronnie went in and shut the door. He walked up a very long passage and found himself in a perfectly round room. He stared in amazement.

A fire with green flames came up from a hole in the middle of the floor! Over it hung a great golden pot in which something boiled and bubbled, singing an odd little tune the whole time. A tall man in a flowing black cloak and a high-pointed hat was pouring something into the pot.

The cat ran up to him and rubbed itself against his legs.

'So you've come back, Cinders!' he said. 'Didn't I tell you not to go out into the fog? You're too late to help me now and I don't feel at all pleased with you.'

'Er – please excuse me,' said Ronnie, feeling puzzled and excited. 'I found your lost cat and brought him back.'

'Oh – I'm sorry I didn't see you,' said the tall man, turning round with a smile that lit up his whole face and made Ronnie like him very much. 'You came in with Cinders, I suppose. Thank you for looking after him. He's no good in a fog, but he will go out in them.'

Ronnie didn't know what to say. He stared at the bubbling pot, and was astonished to see the liquid in it change suddenly from green to yellow and then to a bright silver.

'Excuse me a moment. I really must stir this,' said the man. 'By the way I should introduce myself, shouldn't I? I'm Mr Spells.'

'I'm Ronnie James,' said Ronnie.

'Miaow,' said the cat.

'Don't keep interrupting,' said Mr Spells. 'Oh, you want some milk, do you? Ronnie, stir this mixture for me, will you, and I'll get Cinders some milk.'

Ronnie found himself stirring the strange bubbling mixture. Some of it splashed over the edge of the pot on to his right shoe.

'Oh dear – what a good thing I've got my very oldest shoes on,' said Ronnie. 'Mr Spells – what is this mixture you're making?'

'Oh, just some invisible paint,' said Mr Spells. 'Once it cools, you can use it on anything and it makes any object invisible. You can't see it, you know, when you've dabbed it with this. Very useful sometimes.'

Ronnie began to tremble. Was this man a wizard? His house was called Wizard Cottage – and his name was Mr Spells. He had a black cat too, as all witches and wizards had.

'You needn't be afraid of me,' said Mr Spells kindly. 'I can see you trembling. There are bad wizards and good ones, just as there are bad boys and good boys. Well, I'm a good wizard. I hope you're a good boy?'

'Mother says I am,' said Ronnie, still trembling a little. Then he heard a clock strike five. 'Oh dear – is it really five o'clock? I must go then, because Mother will worry if I don't get back in time. She'll think I'm lost in the fog.'

'Well, thank you again for bringing Cinders home,' said Mr Spells. 'Perhaps you will come and have tea with me tomorrow? I'd be delighted to see you. I could teach you quite a lot of interesting things.'

'Oh, *thank* you! I'd love to come to tea!' said Ronnie, delighted. 'I'll be along at half past four after school.

Goodbye, Mr Spells. Goodbye, Cinders.'

'Miaow,' said Cinders. Ronnie stroked him and then went down the passage and let himself out of the front door. He walked home in the fog, feeling quite dazed. What a very peculiar adventure! And to think he was going to tea with Mr Spells the next day – with a *wizard*! He *must* be a wizard – how very exciting!

His mother laughed when he told her about his adventure. 'You've been dreaming in the fog!' she said. 'But go if you like – and just ask Mr Spells if he can give me a bit of magic to keep the fire from going out. It's behaving very badly lately!'

So the next afternoon Ronnie set off. He went all the way down Hanger Lane to the corner – but dear me, what was this? The house at the corner was called Thornfield, not Wizard Cottage. Then where was Wizard Cottage? It should be next to Thornfield, on the corner.

But it wasn't. There was no house beyond Thornfield. It was a very puzzling thing. No matter how hard Ronnie hunted he simply could not find Wizard Cottage.

Well, all I can think is that Mr Spells must have painted his house with his invisible paint! thought Ronnie. *I'll just have to keep a lookout for old Cinders. I might see him and get him to take me into the house again some day.*

Ronnie's mother wasn't a bit surprised to see Ronnie coming home without having found the house. 'It was all nonsense!' she said. 'You made it up – or dreamt it.'

But now I'll tell you a very peculiar thing. Do you remember that some of the mixture in the pot splashed over on to Ronnie's right shoe? Well, when it cooled it made the whole shoe invisible! So now Ronnie can't see it, and he's been hunting high and low for it.

And it's there in his cupboard, lying beside the left shoe, but it can't be seen! You might tell him, if you see him.

The Wishing Jug

The Wishing Jug

THERE WAS once a poor boy called Tuppeny, who lived with his mother and father in a little tumbledown cottage in the village of Trim. He was a lazy fellow and, instead of doing his work well, he would dream all day long of what he would do if he were a prince instead of a peasant boy.

How fine to live in a castle and have many horses and men of my own, he thought. *I should marry a princess and sit on a throne.*

His work was to scare birds away from the fields. He thought so much about what he would do if he were a prince, that often the birds came and ate the crops under his very nose. Then his master would be very angry with him.

One day, as he sat there twirling his rattle idly in his hands, quite forgetting to shake it at the greedy birds, he talked aloud to himself.

'I should like to wear a red and gold cloak and hang a glittering sword by my side. I should like a feathered cap, and—'

'Well, and why shouldn't you?' said a voice behind him. Tuppeny looked round. He saw behind him a tall, thin man dressed in a cloak with suns, moons and stars all over it. On his head was a pointed hat, and as soon as Tuppeny saw him, he knew that he was a wizard. He jumped up and bowed.

'Have you come to ask me to do anything for you?' he said.

'Well,' said the wizard, 'you might be able to help me out of a difficulty. I have lost the key of my cottage on the hill and I very much want to get something out of it. I believe you could just squeeze in through a little window that has been left open.'

'What will you give me if I do?' asked Tuppeny.

'You shall have the cloak, cap and sword you were wishing for just now!' said the wizard.

'Ho!' said Tuppeny, jumping up and down in delight. 'Lead the way, wizard. I'll climb in through the window for you!'

The wizard led Tuppeny across many fields and at last came to a steep hill. Nestling in the side of it, quite hidden by a clump of trees, was a strange little cottage. Tuppeny had never seen it before – indeed he never remembered seeing the hill either, and puzzled his brains to think how it was that he had missed it.

They came up to the cottage and Tuppeny saw that all the curtains were drawn tightly across the windows. The gate was locked and they had to climb over it. The wizard led the way to where a tiny window at the back had been left open. It was high up, and Tuppeny wondered how he could reach it.

'I'll climb up this pear tree,' he said. 'I think I can just swing myself down to the windowsill if I climb along that branch.'

He swung himself up into the tree and climbed along the branch towards the window. Then in a trice he was on the sill, squeezing his body through the opening.

'Shall I open the front door for you?' he asked the wizard. 'Then you can come in and get what you want.'

'Oh, no, don't bother to do that,' said the wizard. 'All I want is a little red jug you will find in the kitchen in the middle of the table. Just bring me that, there's a good lad.'

Tuppeny ran downstairs into the kitchen. On the table was a little red jug with a carved handle. He picked it up – and then he heard a strange noise from outside. He went to the window and looked out. The wizard was fighting a fierce little gnome!

'What are you doing near my cottage?' cried the

gnome furiously. 'You've come to steal something, I know you have! It's a good thing I locked all my doors. Take that, and that, and that!' shouted the gnome, slapping the wizard hard.

The wizard suddenly cried out a strange word and the gnome disappeared. In his place there came a little whining dog that ran round and round the garden in despair.

Tuppeny was frightened. So this wasn't the wizard's cottage after all! The wizard had sent him to steal the jug. What a wicked man! Tuppeny was quite sure he wouldn't get the cloak and sword he had been promised, and he began to be afraid that the angry wizard would turn him into something too.

So he stole to the back door, slipped back the bolt that fastened it and crept out. He ran to a thick bush and crouched underneath. Soon the wizard went to the window and called him.

'Hurry up, boy!' he shouted. 'Can't you find the jug?'

When he heard no reply he became angry and

shouted more loudly. Suddenly, the little gnome-dog ran up and bit him on the leg, and the wizard gave a scream and fled away down the hill. The gnome-dog ran after him and Tuppeny was left alone under his bush, trembling.

Soon he crept out and ran home as fast as his legs would carry him. When he got there he found that he was carrying the little red jug!

'Ooh!' said Tuppeny in fright. 'I've got the jug! Whatever shall I do with it? I daren't take it back!'

'Where did you get it from?' asked his mother, and he told her. She took it and looked at it.

'Well, it's a pretty little jug,' she said. 'If the gnome comes for it, he can have it – but I'm not going to let you go back to that cottage with it!'

'Let's use it,' said Tuppeny, who thought it was the prettiest jug he had ever seen. 'We'll keep the milk in it, Mother.'

He poured the milk into it and put it on the shelf. When teatime came, his mother set it on the table with the other things. Tuppeny looked to see what there was for tea.

'Only dry bread!' he said in dismay. 'Oh, Mother, what a miserable tea – just the same as breakfast and dinner.'

'Well, times are very hard,' said his mother with a sigh, pouring milk into the cups. 'I wish I had cakes, butter and jam to give you, Tuppeny, but—'

She stopped in surprise – for on the table there suddenly appeared a dish of jam, a dish of yellow butter and two plates of wonderful cakes!

'Ooh!' cried Tuppeny in delight. 'Look at that! Mother, that's a wishing jug, sure as eggs are eggs!'

He snatched it out of his mother's hand and wished again, pouring milk out as he did so, for he guessed that the little jug would not grant wishes unless something was poured out of it at the same time as the wish was wished.

'I wish for a cow of our own, a sheep and a pig!' cried the excited boy.

'Moo!', 'Baa!', 'Grunt!' came from behind him, and there in the kitchen stood the three animals he had wished for! His mother cried out in astonishment and drove them into the yard.

'Be careful what you wish for, you silly boy,' she said. 'I don't want my little kitchen crowded out with farm animals.'

'I wish for a big kitchen!' cried Tuppeny. 'I wish for a big house! I wish for a garden, and a farm, and an orchard!'

In a twinkling, the kitchen became a great, big, shining room with an enormous stove at one end. The cottage disappeared and a grand house arose in its place. The tiny garden became spacious grounds, and in the distance, fields appeared dotted with sheep, horses and cows. A fine orchard came not far away, its trees laden with ripe fruit.

'My goodness!' shouted Tuppeny in delight. 'We're rich! We're grand! I can be a prince and marry a princess!'

74

The jug was empty by this time, so Tuppeny filled it with water and began pouring it out, wishing all the time.

'I wish for a suit of red and gold,' he said, 'and a feathered cap and flowing cloak. I want a glittering sword and a horse with nodding plumes. I want a hundred servants to follow me, each carrying a sack of gold or jewels. Ha, I'll be the grandest person in the land. I'll go tomorrow and ask for the hand of Princess Melanie and marry her!'

As he wished, each wish came true. He was clad in red and gold and a horse with nodding plumes appeared in the garden. A hundred servants walked up the broad path, each carrying a blue sack which Tuppeny guessed to be full of gold or jewels.

'Sleep in the garden,' he commanded them with a wave of his hand. 'I shall not need you till tomorrow.' The men obediently sank down on the grass and went to sleep. Tuppeny and his mother talked excitedly till his father came home, and stared in wonder at the great house that stood in the place of his cottage. Tuppeny ran out and dragged him indoors, and the astonished man looked at the little red jug that had worked such wonders.

The next day, Tuppeny set out to go to the palace of the king! He rode on his beautiful black horse, and a glittering sword hung by his side. His cloak of red and gold streamed out in the wind, and behind him walked his hundred servants with their sacks.

At midday, he arrived at the palace gates and the sentries opened them to let in this magnificent youth with his great following.

'Tell His Majesty that Prince Tuppeny of Trim has come to see him,' said the bold youth. The king, hearing how grand the youth looked, and what a number of servants he had, commanded him to be brought before him.

'Your Majesty, I have come to ask for your daughter's hand,' said Tuppeny, bowing low.

The king laughed.

'I know nothing of you,' he said. 'Where do you come from?'

'From the great land of Trim,' answered Tuppeny. 'I have brought some presents for you, sire.'

His hundred servants came forward and emptied their sacks in front of the throne. The king stared in amazement. He had never seen so much gold, nor so many glittering jewels before. *This must be a very rich prince*, he thought!

The Princess Melanie was sitting beside her father. She was a pretty maiden and she liked the look of Tuppeny. He was much nicer looking than the old duke that her father had chosen for her to marry. She liked his merry, black eyes and curly hair.

'I'd like to marry this prince,' she said. Tuppeny blushed with pleasure.

The king bade his daughter be silent.

'My daughter is already promised in marriage to the Duke of Waitabit,' he said. 'He has a castle ready for her and a necklace of lovely diamonds.'

'I will build her ten palaces, each lovelier than the other!' cried Tuppeny. 'I will give her a hundred necklaces, a thousand brooches and as many dresses as she pleases to have!'

'Nonsense!' said the king. 'No one is rich enough for that. If you could do as you say, I might give you my daughter, but such words are empty as air.'

'Will you give me the Princess Melanie to be my wife if I build her ten palaces tonight?' asked Tuppeny eagerly.

'Yes!' said the king, laughing. 'I know quite well that such a thing can never be done. But listen, boy – if you fail, I shall clap you in prison for a year! That will teach you to boast idly!'

Tuppeny bowed and went out. He took the little red jug from the leather bag in which he carried it, and filled it with water from a pump. Then he wished.

'I wish that ten palaces, each more beautiful than the last, may appear before the king's eyes tomorrow morning,' he said. 'And I wish that a hundred pages shall appear before the Princess Melanie carrying necklaces and brooches made of the most precious stones in the world, and that twenty maidens shall also appear, bringing with them dresses made of silks and satins, embroidered with silver and gold.'

The next day, Tuppeny went to the palace very early, and asked to be shown into the king's presence as soon as he was up. When the king at last received him, he bowed to the floor.

'Your Majesty,' he said, 'I come to claim the Princess Melanie. I would marry her today.'

'Nonsense!' said the king sharply. 'Don't be foolish. Where are these wonderful palaces you boasted of? Be off before I keep my word and clap you into prison.'

'Your Majesty, pray come to the window,' said Tuppeny. The king went to the window and leant out. At that very moment the wonder happened. One by one, ten gleaming palaces arose out of nothing, and stood round the king's own palace, glittering in their beauty, their towers and spires rising high in the sunlit air.

Then, from each palace came ten pages carrying splendid necklaces and brooches on cushions of black velvet. Following them came the maidens with wonderful dresses for the delighted Princess Melanie who flung her arms round Tuppeny and kissed him.

'I shall marry you today!' she declared. 'You are the most wonderful youth in the world! Oh, Father, think of having ten lovely palaces for my own, and all those jewels and dresses!'

'Well, I hope that your husband will kindly plant the palaces a little further off,' said the king. 'They are very magnificent, but they spoil my view. Stop hugging Prince Tuppeny, Melanie, and go and get ready for your marriage. I suppose I must keep my word and give you to the prince.'

What a to-do there was that day! The princess was married to Tuppeny, and all the people cheered madly when they saw the handsome pair driving through the streets in a carriage made of pure gold, drawn by twenty coal-black horses, each with a white star in the middle of its forehead. Tuppeny had wished for this, and the princess was simply delighted.

The next thing that Tuppeny did was to move the ten palaces a little further away, each on a hill which he had specially made for them. Then he and the Princess Melanie stayed a week in each one in turn, enjoying life very much indeed.

Tuppeny gave Melanie the wishing jug for a wedding present, and at first she used it every day, finding it great fun to have all her wishes come true, no matter what they were. Then she grew tired of it, and put it away in the china cupboard, forgetting all about it, for she had every single thing she wanted.

One day a beggar came to the kitchen door, and begged for a glass of water.

'Get it yourself from the pump in the yard,' said the maid rudely.

'Lend me a jug to get it with,' said the man. The

maid opened the door of the china cupboard and looked for an old jug to give him.

'That red one will do,' said the man, and the maid gave it to him. As soon as he had it in his hands, he gave a loud laugh and ran to the pump. It was the wizard! He filled the jug with water and began to wish. He wished the palaces to become cottages, and all Tuppeny's lovely horses to become mice. He wished and wished and wished, and Tuppeny couldn't think what was happening around him, for everything began to change as the wizard wished.

At last Tuppeny rushed out to see what was the matter – and there in the yard he saw the wizard who had sent him into the gnome's cottage to steal the red jug!

He saw the jug in the wizard's hand and rushed at him. He snatched at it, and the two began to wrestle for it. There was still a little water in it, and the wizard tried to pour it out and wish at the same time, but Tuppeny wouldn't let him.

'Give me the jug!' cried Tuppeny, hitting the wizard on the head.

'Ooh!' shouted the wizard in pain. 'All right – you shall have the jug!'

He managed to pour out a little water and wished as he did so.

'I wish you away in a desert land!' he cried. 'And much good may the wishing jug do you there!'

In a trice Tuppeny had disappeared. He flew through the air and at last landed with a bump on yellow sand. All around him stretched a desolate country. Here and there were low bushes and stunted trees, but not a man or woman was to be seen.

'Well, never mind, I've got the wishing jug!' said Tuppeny. 'I'll just wish myself home again and put everything right once more.'

But alas, the jug was empty! It would not grant wishes unless something was poured out of it, and Tuppeny looked around for a stream or pond. But in that desolate country there was none.

All that day and the next poor Tuppeny wandered on and on looking for some water, but could find none.

'I shall die of thirst!' he groaned. 'If it were not for these fruits that grow on the bushes, I should be dead already, the sun is so hot.'

That night Tuppeny lay down to sleep in despair. He knew there was no water to be found – but in the night he awoke suddenly. Something soft and wet was falling on his face.

'It's raining!' cried Tuppeny in joy. 'It's raining! Where's my jug?'

He stood out in the rain – but the shower was soon over and there were very few drops in the jug.

Tuppeny poured them out and wished quickly before the jug was empty, wondering if the tiny amount of water was enough for a wish.

'I wish myself outside the pump at home!' he cried.

Yes! There was just enough water for a wish, for Tuppeny found himself flying through the air at a great pace and at last landed on his feet just beside the pump from which the wizard had filled the jug. Quickly Tuppeny filled it full, and wished loudly.

'Let everything be as it was two days ago!' he said – and hey presto, the palaces came back with a rush, the mice became horses, the princess came rushing down the steps, and Tuppeny shouted aloud in delight. Everything was as it was before.

'This jug is too dangerous to be left about,' said Tuppeny, after he had hugged his Melanie. 'If that wizard ever gets it again, we shall be in a bad way! Listen, darling Melanie – have you everything you want?'

'Everything!' said the princess.

'So have I!' said Tuppeny. 'So I'll smash the jug and no one can ever wish us ill!'

He threw the little red jug on the ground and it smashed into a hundred pieces. Each piece turned green, gave out a little spire of smoke and vanished.

'Ooh!' said Princess Melanie. 'Did you see that?'

Tuppeny laughed. 'I want a drink of lemonade,' he said. 'I'm dreadfully thirsty!'

'I'll get you some,' said Melanie. 'But, Tuppeny, I'm sorry you broke the jug – it would have been such fun to show it to our children and let them wish.'

'We'll get the story of it written down for everyone to read!' said Tuppeny. 'I'm sure they'll like it!'

And I hope you did!

The Moon in the Pail

The Moon in the Pail

ONE NIGHT the moon was full. It hung in the sky like a great white globe and shone marvellously.

'I wonder who hung that lamp in the sky tonight,' said Bobs, the black-and-white fox terrier. 'It's lighting up the whole garden. It's wonderful. I like it.'

'Do you see how it sails in and out of the clouds?' said Cosy, the tabby cat. 'I'd like to do that. It would be fun.'

'I wish I had the moon for my own,' said Topsy, the fox terrier puppy. 'I would like such a lovely thing to play with. I would roll it down the garden path and it would give me light wherever it went. Oh, I do wish I had it.'

'I'll get it for you,' said Bimbo, the naughty Siamese kitten, grinning. 'What will you give me if I do?'

'I'll give you the big bone that the butcher boy threw to me this morning,' said Topsy, after she had thought for a while. 'That's what I'll give you. I've hidden it away and nobody knows where it is. But I'll give it to you if you really will get me the moon to play with.'

'Right!' said Bimbo, and ran off. He came to where the cook had stood an empty pail outside the kitchen door. He dragged it to the garden tap and filled the pail full of water.

The reflection of the bright moon shone in the pail of water. It looked lovely there, round and bright, just like the moon in the sky.

Bimbo waited until the water was quite still, and the moon shone there, round and beautiful. Then he ran off to find Topsy.

'Topsy!' he mewed. 'I've got the moon for you. Come and see.'

'Oh, where?' cried Topsy in delight, and ran off with Bimbo to the pail.

'Look in my pail of water,' said Bimbo. 'Do you see the moon there? Well, you can have it.'

'Yes, it's really there,' said Topsy, looking at the reflection of the bright moon there. It really did look exactly as if the moon had fallen into the pail! 'Oh, Bimbo, how good and clever you are to get me the moon, as I asked. But why did you put it into a pail of water?'

'Well, it might have got out if it hadn't got water over it,' said Bimbo at once. 'Now, Topsy, remember your promise – where's that big bone you hid away?'

'I'll show you,' said Topsy, and she took Bimbo to where the yew hedge grew. She dug about a little and sniffed. Then she began to scrabble and scrape for all she was worth, and at last, up came the great big juicy bone that the butcher boy had given to Topsy. It was rather dirty, but Bimbo didn't mind that! He took it in his mouth and ran off.

'You go and play with your moon!' said Bimbo with a laugh. So off Topsy went to the pail of water.

The moon still swam there, round and bright. Topsy sat down and looked into the water. 'Come on out, Moon,' she said. 'I want to play with you. Come out, and I will roll you down the path like a big shining ball, and every little mouse and hedgehog, every beetle and worm, will come out to watch you rolling by!'

But the moon didn't come out. It stayed in the pail and shone there, silvery bright.

'Do come out!' begged Topsy. 'Please do. It must be so nasty and cold there in the water, and so wet too. That's the horrid thing about water, it's always so wet. If it was dry, it would be much nicer to bathe in.'

The moon shone there, but it didn't come out. Topsy grew angry.

'Do you want me to put my nose into the water and get you out?' she barked. 'You won't like that. I might nip you with my teeth, Moon. Come along out, do!'

But the moon didn't. Topsy sat and looked at it, with her head on one side. 'Well, I shall put in my nose then,' she said. 'And I shall get hold of you. So look out!'

She put her nose into the water and tried to get hold of the moon. But, of course, the moon wasn't really there, so all that poor Topsy got was a mouthful of water that made her choke and cough. She was very angry.

'Do you know what I am going to do?' she wuffed. 'I am going to tip the pail over, then the water will run out and away, and you will find yourself on the ground for me to play with!'

So Topsy tipped over the pail and out went the water with a gurgling noise all over the ground. Topsy waited to jump on the moon, but what a peculiar thing – no moon came out of the pail!

'Where's it gone, where's it gone?' howled Topsy, scraping about the ground as if she thought the moon was stuck there. 'She was in the water and the water's out, but the moon isn't.'

'Whatever is the matter?' said Bobs, wandering up. 'What are you doing dancing round that empty pail, Topsy? Have you suddenly gone mad?'

'No,' said Topsy. 'But a very sad thing has happened, Bobs. Bimbo got the moon and put her into a pail of water for me. I tipped up the pail to get the moon out, but somehow she's slipped away and gone. I can't find her.'

'Well, I know where she's gone,' said Bobs with a sudden giggle.

'Where?' said Topsy in surprise.

'Back to the sky. Look!' said Bobs. And when Topsy looked up into the sky, sure enough there was the bright round moon sailing along between the clouds as quickly as ever!

'Well! To think she jumped back there so quickly!'

said Topsy in surprise. 'Bimbo! Bimbo! Give me back my bone! The moon's got out of the pail and has gone back to the sky!'

But Bimbo was nowhere to be found. Neither was the bone! I'm not at all surprised, are you?

The Enchanted Shoes

The Enchanted Shoes

ONCE UPON a time there was a boy called William, who lived with his mother at the foot of some high hills. Nobody lived up on the hills for it was said that dwarfs lived in caves there, and no one liked to walk on the sunny hillside.

William's mother often warned him not to go wandering in the hills, and to beware of any strange thing that he saw for fear it was enchanted.

But William saw nothing at all, and he wasn't a bit afraid of dwarfs, no, nor giants either. Not he!

One day he went to look for wild strawberries at the foot of the hills. They were hard to find, but just as he was about to give up, he suddenly saw a sunny bank a little way up the hill, where he was quite certain he would find some. To get there he had to cross a very boggy piece of ground – and dear me, before he knew what was happening he was sinking right down in it!

Quickly, William slipped off his heavy boots, which were held tightly in the mud, and leapt lightly to a dry tuft of grass.

'Bother!' he cried. 'I've lost my boots! I shall get thorns and prickles in my feet if I'm not careful.'

Then he saw a strange sight – for on a flat dry stone just in front of him there was a pair of smart red shoes with silver buckles! William stared at them in surprise. Who could they belong to? He looked around but he couldn't see anyone.

'Hallo! Is anybody about?' William shouted loudly. 'Whose shoes are these?' But there was no answer at all.

William looked at the shoes again. It seemed a pity

not to borrow them when he had none. He wouldn't spoil them – he would just wear them home and then try to find out who the owner was.

So he picked up the shoes and slipped them on his feet. They fitted him exactly.

William thought they looked very nice. He stood up and tried them. Yes, they really might have been made for him!

I'd better go back down the hill, he thought suddenly. *I've come too far up, and Mother always warns me not to.*

He turned to go back down – but to his surprise his feet walked the other way! Yes, they walked up the hill, instead of down!

William couldn't believe it. Here he was trying to walk down the hill and he couldn't. He tried to force his feet to turn round but it was no good at all! They simply wouldn't!

'Oh no!' said William. 'Why did I meddle with these shoes? I might have guessed they were magic! I've got to go where the shoes take me, I suppose.

I wonder, though, if I could take them off.'

But his feet wouldn't stop walking long enough for him to try, so on he had to go. Up the hill his feet took him, along a steep path, and up to a small yellow door in the hillside.

As he came up to it, the door opened and a little dwarf, dressed in red and yellow, looked out. He grinned when he saw William.

'Ha! My shoes have caught someone at last. Good!'

'You've no right to lay traps like that,' said William crossly, as his feet took him through the door. 'Take these shoes off my feet at once!'

'Oh, no, my fine fellow!' said the dwarf, chuckling. 'Now I've got you, I'm going to keep you. It's no good trying to get those shoes off – they're stuck on by magic, and only magic will get them off!'

'Well, what are you going to do with me?' asked William.

'I want an errand boy,' said the dwarf. 'I do lots of

business with witches, wizards and giants, sending out all sorts of spells and charms, and I want someone to deliver them for me.'

'I don't see why I should work for you!' said William. 'I want to go home.'

'How dare you talk to me like that!' cried the dwarf, flying into a rage. 'I'll turn you into a frog!'

'All right, all right!' said William with a sigh. 'But I shall escape as soon as I possibly can.'

'Not as long as you've got those shoes on,' said the dwarf with a grin. 'They will always bring you back to me, no matter where you go!'

Poor William. He had to start on his new job straight away.

The dwarf wrapped up a strange little blue flower in a piece of yellow paper and told William to take it to Witch Twiddle. The shoes started off at once and, puffing and panting, William climbed right to the top of the hill where he found a small cottage, half tumbling down. Green smoke came from the chimney and from inside came a high, chanting voice. It was the witch singing a spell.

'Come in!' she called when William knocked at the door. He went inside and found Witch Twiddle stirring a big black pot over a small fire. She was singing strings of magic words and William stood open-mouthed, watching.

'What are you gaping at, you nincompoop?' said the witch impatiently.

'I'm not a nincompoop!' exclaimed William. 'It's just that I've never seen boiling water send up green steam before!'

'Then you are a nincompoop!' said the witch. 'What have you come here for anyway?'

'I've come from the dwarf down the hill,' said William. 'He sent you this.'

He held out the little yellow package and the witch pounced on it greedily.

'Ha! The spell he said he would give me! Good!' William wanted to sit down and have a rest, but the enchanted shoes walked him out of the cottage and down the hill again.

Trimble the dwarf was waiting for him with a heap of small packages to deliver.

'Look here!' said William firmly. 'I'm not going to take all those. I want a rest.'

'Well, you'll have to do without one,' said the dwarf. 'I want these packages delivered. This goes to Wizard Cast-a-Spell, and this to Dwindle the dwarf, and this to Rumble the giant.'

'But I don't know where they live,' said William.

'That doesn't matter,' said Trimble. 'The enchanted shoes will take you there!'

And so they did. It was most peculiar. First they took him to a little wood, in the middle of which was a very high tower with no door. A neat little notice said: CAST-A-SPELL THE WIZARD.

'That's funny,' said William looking all around. 'There's no way to get in!'

He knocked on the wall of the tower.

'Come in, come in!' cried a voice.

'How?' asked William. 'There's no door.'

'Oh, bless me if I haven't forgotten to put the door back again!' said a grumbling voice from inside. 'Come back, door!'

At once a bright green door appeared in the tower.

William stared at it, astonished. Then he opened it and stepped into a small, round room where a hunched-up old man sat reading an enormous book. His beard was so long and thick that it spread all over the floor. William had to take care not to tread on it.

'Here you are,' said William. 'It's a parcel from Trimble the dwarf.'

William gave the old man the package and left. To his surprise, the door vanished as soon as he was outside. It was most peculiar.

His enchanted shoes would not let him stay for a moment. They ran him out of the wizard's wood and took him halfway down the other side of the hill before they stopped.

'What's the matter now?' wondered William. 'I can't see any house. These shoes have made a mistake. I hope they won't keep me out here in the cold all day!'

Just then the earth began to shake beneath his feet! He felt frightened, and wondered if there was an earthquake. Then suddenly he heard a cross little voice.

'Get off my front door! I can't open it. Get off, I say!'

The voice seemed to come from down below. William felt the earth shaking under him again and then, to his astonishment, he saw that he was standing on a neat brown trapdoor, just the colour of the hillside! On the trapdoor was a little nameplate that said: DWINDLE THE DWARF.

'I'm so sorry!' called William. There was an angry noise below. Then suddenly someone pushed the trapdoor open so hard that William was sent flying into the air and fell down with a bump.

'Careful!' shouted William crossly. 'You sent me flying!'

'Serves you right,' said the bad-tempered dwarf, sticking his head out of the open trapdoor. 'What do you want here, anyway? Are you the boy that brings the potatoes?'

'No, I am not!' said William. 'I've been sent by Trimble the dwarf to bring you this package.'

The dwarf snatched the parcel from his hand and disappeared down the trapdoor at once, slamming it shut behind him.

'Go away,' he called. 'And don't you ever stand on my door again.'

At once, William's enchanted shoes took him back up the hill at a fast trot.

'I've only got to go to Giant Rumble now,' said William. 'Thank goodness! I feel quite exhausted!'

Soon he came to something that looked like a big golden pole. As he got near it, he saw that it was a long, long ladder of gold, reaching up into the sky and into a large black cloud.

His feet began to climb up the ladder, and dear me, it was very hard work! Before he was very far up he badly wanted a rest – but the enchanted shoes wouldn't stop. Up and up they went!

After a long while William reached the top. He looked round and saw an extraordinary palace, which seemed to be made entirely of mist.

'This doesn't look as if it is the home of a giant,' said William to himself. 'It's big enough – but it doesn't seem strong enough! It's all so soft and misty!'

But all the same, a giant did live there. The front door opened as William drew near, and inside he saw a great hall, higher than the highest tree he had ever seen. Sitting at a carved table was a giant with a broad, kindly face. He looked down smilingly at the boy as he walked forward. 'Where do you come from, boy?' he asked.

'From Trimble the dwarf,' answered William. 'He sent you this parcel.'

'About time too,' said the giant, stretching out such an enormous hand for it that William felt quite frightened. 'Don't be afraid, my boy. I won't hurt you. I'm a cloud-giant and I live up here to make the thunder you hear sometimes. But I do no harm to anyone.'

The giant opened the parcel and then frowned angrily. 'The dwarf has sent me the wrong spell again!' he grumbled. 'Do you know anything about spells, boy?'

'Nothing at all,' said William.

'Dear me, that's a pity,' said Rumble. 'I'm doing a summer-thunder spell, and I've got to multiply twelve lightning flashes by eleven thunder claps. I don't know the answer. Trimble said he'd send it to me, but he hasn't, I'm sure.'

'What does he say the answer is?' asked William, who knew his tables very well indeed.

'He says that twelve flashes of lightning multiplied by eleven claps of thunder make ninety-nine storm clouds,' said Rumble.

'Quite wrong,' said William. 'Twelve times eleven is one hundred and thirty-two.'

'Well, is that so?' said the giant. 'I am pleased! Now I can do my spell. I'm really very much obliged to you. I suppose I can't possibly do anything for you in return?'

'Well, yes, you can,' said William at once. 'You can tell me how to get rid of these shoes.'

'Well, the only way to get rid of them is to put them on someone else,' said Rumble. 'Tell me who you'd like to put them on and I'll tell you how to get them off!'

'I'd like to make that horrible little dwarf Trimble wear them, and send him off to the moon!' said William.

'Ha, ha, ha, ha!' laughed the giant. 'Best joke I've heard for years! That would serve him right. Now listen. Wait till the dwarf is asleep, and then slip these tiny stones into your shoes. You will find that they come off at once. Put them on Trimble's feet before you can count ten, and tell him where to go. He'll go all right! The shoes will start him walking and he'll never come back.'

'Oh, thank you,' said William gratefully, and took the small pebbles that Rumble gave him. He said goodbye to the kindly giant and then climbed quickly down the ladder.

He was soon back at Trimble's house and found him having his dinner. The dwarf threw the boy a crust dipped in gravy and told him that as soon as he had finished eating there were some more errands to do.

'I'm going to have my after-dinner nap,' he said, lying down on a sofa. 'Wake me when you've finished cleaning up.'

William was too excited even to eat his crust. As soon as he heard Trimble snoring loudly, William slipped the magic pebbles into the shoes. They came off as easily as could be, and in great delight he ran over to Trimble. As soon as the shoes were off, William began to count.

'One, two, three,' he counted, as he began to slip the shoes on to Trimble's feet – but to his horror the dwarf's feet were far too large – twice the size of William's! Whatever could he do?

'Four, five, six, seven, eight, nine—' he continued to count in despair, for the shoes certainly would not go on the dwarf's feet. And then, at the very last moment William had an idea. He would put them on the dwarf's hands!

He fitted them on quickly, counting 'Ten!' as he did so – and at the same moment the dwarf awoke!

'What are you doing?' he cried angrily, jumping up. 'I'll turn you into a frog, I'll—'

'Walk to the moon!' shouted William in excitement – and then a most extraordinary thing happened! For the dwarf suddenly stood on his hands and began to walk on them out of his cottage! Trimble was even more astonished than William.

'Mercy! Mercy!' he cried. 'Take these shoes off.'

'I don't know how to,' said William. 'But anyway, it serves you right. Go on, shoes – walk to the moon and then, if the dwarf has repented of his bad ways, you may bring him back again!'

The dwarf was soon a long way off, walking upside down on his hands, weeping and wailing.

As soon as the dwarf was out of sight, a crowd of little folk came running up to William. They were dressed in red and green tunics and had bright, happy faces.

'We are the hill brownies,' they said, 'and we've come to thank you for punishing that horrible dwarf. Now we shall all be happy, and you and your friends can walk safely up the hillside. Ho ho! Wasn't it a surprise for Trimble to be sent walking to the moon on his hands! That was very clever of you.'

The jolly little hill brownies took William safely back home and even fetched his lost boots for him out of the bog into which they had sunk. And now William and his friends walk unafraid all over the hills, for the friendly brownies are about now and the nasty dwarfs have fled, frightened by the fate of Trimble.

As for Trimble, he hasn't even walked halfway to the moon yet, so goodness knows when he'll be back!

The Little Brownie
House

The Little Brownie House

KIM AND MICKLE were very worried. They were brownies who lived in a treehouse – and now the woodman had come to chop down their tree.

'We shall have to move,' said Kim. 'And quickly too, or the tree will come down and all our furniture with it! Hurry, Mickle, and get it all out.'

So the brownies took their furniture on their shoulders and piled it on the grass below. There it stood, and there the brownies stood too, wondering where to go.

They borrowed a handcart from Bonny the pixie and put the furniture on it, ready to wheel away.

But there really seemed nowhere at all to go. There had been so many old trees cut down in the wood that other people had taken all the empty houses there were.

'There's not even a hole in a bank we can have,' said Kim. 'At least, there's one – but the fox lives there and he doesn't smell very nice.'

'Oh, we can't go there,' said Mickle. 'We'd have to hold our noses all the time!'

'Well, let's wheel our barrow around a bit and see if there's any empty house we can go to,' said Kim. So, with the noise of the woodman's axe ringing in their ears, they wheeled their cart away, with their two little beds, their two little chairs, their table, cupboard, curtains and mats on it, looking rather forlorn.

They came at last to a high hedge. At the bottom was a gap, so they wheeled the barrow through – and there in a garden was a little empty house! It was painted brown and had a big open doorway.

'I say! Look at this!' cried Kim, running to it. 'An empty house – just our size too! What about living here? There's nothing in the house at all, except some old straw.'

'It's fine,' said Mickle. 'But it's rather a funny house, Kim – there's no door – and no window either!'

'Well, that doesn't matter, Mickle!' said Kim. 'We can easily make a door and just as easily make a window! Oh, Mickle – it will be fun living in this little house, won't it!'

Well, the two brownies moved in. The house was exactly right for them. They put in their beds, one on each side of the room, for the house had only the one room. 'Our beds can do for couches in the daytime,' said Kim.

They put the table in the middle and the chairs beside it. They put the cupboard at the back and spread the rugs on the floor. You can't think how lovely it all looked when it was done.

They had a tiny jam jar and Kim went to fetch some

daisies for it. He put the vase of daisies in the middle of the table.

Mickle put the clock on the cupboard and wound it up. Tick-tick-tock-tock! it went.

'There now!' said Kim. 'Flowers on the table – and a clock ticking. It's home, real home, isn't it!'

The brownies were very happy. The little house looked out on to a garden belonging to a big house built of brick. People lived there and two children often came out of the house to play. But they never came to the brownies' house.

'It's a good thing our house is right at the bottom of the garden, where nobody ever comes,' said Kim. 'Now, Mickle – what about making a door? The rain came in yesterday and wetted the mats.'

So the two brownies set about making a door. They found a nice piece of wood and with their tools they made it just the right size for a door. They painted it blue and hung it on the doorway with two little brass hinges. It opened and shut beautifully.

They put a knocker on it and made a slit for a letterbox. It did look nice.

'And now we'd better make two little windows,' said Mickle. 'When we have the door shut, our house is very dark and stuffy. We will make a little window each side and find some glass to put in.'

So they carved out two squares for windows, and found some broken glass by the garden frames. They cut two pieces to the right size and fitted them in. Then they cleaned the windows and hung up blue curtains.

'Really, it looks simply lovely now!' said Kim. 'The door is such a nice blue and the knocker shines so brightly, and the curtains at the windows look so pretty. I think we ought to have a party.'

'Yes, we ought,' said Mickle. 'But if we give a party, we must make cakes. And we can't bake cakes unless we have an oven and a chimney – and there isn't a chimney, you know.'

So they made a chimney and bought a nice little

oven from the pixie down the way. They fixed it into the corner and then lit a fire. The smoke went straight up the chimney and away into the garden. It was marvellous! The oven cooked beautifully, and what a delicious smell came from it the first time that the brownies cooked buns and cakes!

They sent out the invitations to the party. 'Everyone will love our little house,' said Kim. 'They will think we are very, very lucky to have found it. I do wonder who it belonged to. We have never heard.'

Now, on the day of the party, Kim and Mickle began to do a great cleaning and cooking. All the mats were shaken, the windows were cleaned, the knocker was polished and the stove cooked cakes, buns and biscuits without stopping. It was great fun.

And then something extraordinary happened! A voice outside the house cried out, 'Look at this! There's somebody living here!'

The brownies peeped out of the window and saw two children, a boy and a girl, staring in the greatest astonishment at their house. 'Goodness!' said Mickle. 'Do you suppose it's *their* house and they want to come back and live in it? Oh dear, I do hope they won't turn us out!'

'We'd better go and ask them,' said Kim. But before he could do that, somebody knocked at the door. They used the little knocker – rat-a-tat-tat! Kim opened the door. He saw the two children looking down at him in delight and surprise.

'Hallo!' said the boy. 'Do you really live here?'

'Yes,' said Kim. 'I hope you don't mind. It was empty when we found it, and there was nobody to say who it belonged to. Do *you* want to come and live here?'

The children laughed and laughed. 'No, you funny little thing!' said the girl. 'Of course we don't. We live in that big house up the garden.'

'Oh, then this isn't your house?' said Kim.

'It used to be our dog's kennel,' said the boy with a giggle. 'But we don't keep a dog now, so the kennel has been empty for a long time. Today we saw smoke at the bottom of the garden and we came down to see what it was. And we suddenly saw a chimney on our dog's kennel and two little windows, and a front door with a knocker!'

'We *did* get a surprise!' said the girl. 'But oh, it's simply lovely! You have made the kennel into the dearest, prettiest little house I ever saw in my life!'

'So it was your dog's kennel!' said Mickle. 'Oh, I do hope you won't want it for another dog.'

'No, Mummy says dogs bark too much,' said the boy. 'So you're quite safe.'

'May we really go on living here then?' asked Kim.

'Of course,' said the girl. 'We'll never tell anyone about you, we promise. But please, please may we sometimes come down, knock at your door and talk to you? You know, it's *awfully* exciting to have a brownie house at the bottom of our garden, with real brownies living there.'

'You *are* nice,' said Mickle. 'Listen – we're having a party this afternoon. Would you like to come? You can't get inside the house comfortably, I'm afraid, but you could eat buns and biscuits out on the grass.'

The two children squealed with joy. 'Oh, *yes*!' said the girl. 'Do, do let us come. We shall see all your friends then. And oh, little brownie, would you like me to lend you my best doll's tea set for the party? It's very pretty, with a blue-and-yellow pattern.'

'Thank you very much,' said Mickle. 'We haven't really got enough cups and plates and we'd love to borrow yours.'

So they borrowed the tea set and it looked fine in the little brownie house, set out on the round table. The party was simply lovely – but the two who enjoyed it most were the children, as you can guess. It was such a treat to sit and look at all the little folk coming to the dog's kennel, dressed in their best, knocking at the blue door and saying, 'How do you do?' to Mickle and Kim!

I won't tell you the names of the children, in case you know them – because they don't want anyone else to visit the brownie house and frighten away their tiny friends. But don't you think they're lucky to have a dog kennel that is used by Mickle and Kim? Wouldn't I just love to visit there!

The Wizard's Needle

The Wizard's Needle

THERE WAS once a wizard called So-So, who had a wonderful needle. He had only to speak to it and it would start sewing anything he wanted.

If he said, 'Needle, make me a bag,' it would make one.

If he said, 'Needle, make me a coat,' it would at once set to work to make him one out of any old rag.

Now one day Curly-Toes the pixie wanted some sacks for his potatoes. He couldn't afford to buy any, so he thought he would make them out of some old pieces of carpet that he had got. But when he had finished making one sack, he was very tired indeed, for he hated sewing.

If only I could borrow So-So's needle, he thought, *how fine that would be! I should only say, 'Needle, make me a sack,' and it would make me one at once. All I should have to do would be to sit and watch it!*

He made up his mind to go to Wizard So-So's and ask him for the loan of his magic needle. So he put on his hat and set out. He banged at So-So's door and the wizard opened it.

'Will you lend me your magic needle?' asked Curly-Toes.

'Certainly not,' said So-So. 'I never lend it to anyone. It is far too valuable.'

He slammed the door and left Curly-Toes on the step, frowning hard.

The pixie was setting off home again when he happened to catch sight of the needle on a table just inside So-So's kitchen window.

Ho! he thought. *There's the needle itself! What's to prevent me from taking it and using it without the wizard*

*knowing? I can easily put it back again when I have finished
with it and he won't be any the wiser!*

With that, the naughty pixie slipped his hand
through the open window, picked up the needle, and
ran off! It wasn't long before he was home again.

He took all the pieces of old carpet and laid them in
a row on the floor. Then he put the magic needle in the
middle of them.

'Needle, make me some sacks!' he said.

At once the little needle got busy. It jumped to a
piece of carpet, and in a trice it had sewn one piece
into a fine sack.

There was a long thread always sticking out of the
needle and it used this to sew the sack together. It was
really wonderful to watch.

Curly-Toes enjoyed it all thoroughly.

It was fine to sit down at the table and see the needle
doing all his hard work. He would have plenty of
strong sacks for his potatoes.

In five minutes the needle had used up all the pieces

of carpet and had made six good sacks.

Curly-Toes waited for it to put itself quietly down beside them, then he meant to pick it up again and take it back to So-So's house.

But the needle didn't stop sewing! To Curly-Toes' great surprise it whipped up the lovely new rug on the floor and began to make a sack of that too!

'Hey!' said Curly-Toes angrily. 'Stop, needle! That's my new rug! Don't spoil it! I don't want any more sacks now.'

The needle took no notice at all. It just went on sewing the rug into a sack. Curly-Toes rushed up to it and tried to stop it. It pricked him hard on the finger and he howled with pain.

'Oh, you horrid needle!' he wept. 'Why don't you stop when you're told to? Stop, I tell you, stop!'

The needle still took no notice. It finished making a sack of the rug and then whipped down one of Curly-Toes' pretty red curtains and began to make that into a sack too.

The pixie couldn't bear it. He had made the curtains himself and he wasn't going to have them all spoilt.

He took a pair of pincers and went softly up to the needle. He suddenly pounced on it and caught it in the pincers. But it wasn't any good at all!

The needle slipped out quite easily and gave the pixie such a jab in the arm that he danced round the room in pain.

The needle took down the other curtain and made a sack of that too. Then it hopped on to the table and Curly-Toes gave a cry of rage.

It was going to make his lovely blue tablecloth into a sack as well!

'You shan't, you shan't!' he cried. 'I had it for my birthday and you shan't spoil it!'

He climbed on to the table and sat himself firmly down in the middle of the cloth to stop the needle from making it into a sack. But it wasn't a bit of good!

In a trice, the cloth was being sewn into a sack – and, oh dear me, what was happening?

Curly-Toes suddenly found himself sewn tightly into the sack too! The needle pulled the neck of the sack tight and sewed it carefully all the way round. Then it flew out of the window!

Poor Curly-Toes! He sat in the middle of the table, sewn tightly into a sack made of his blue tablecloth.

He struggled and wriggled, shouted and cried. But he couldn't get out of that sack!

Soon his friends heard his cries and they came running to his aid. How they laughed to see the pixie in such a fix!

They got some scissors and tried to cut the stitches open round the neck of the sack. But they couldn't! The thread was magic and, try as they would, they couldn't cut it or break it.

'Well, Curly-Toes, this is a fine thing!' said his friends. 'We can't set you free! You will have to go to Wizard So-So's and ask him to help you. Come along, we will go with you.'

So poor Curly-Toes was helped off the table and

then he hopped slowly out of his front door, for it was impossible to walk in the sack.

He could do nothing but jump.

He kept tumbling over and, really, it was the funniest sight, though the pixie didn't think so.

At last he arrived at the wizard's house, and So-So opened the door. How he laughed to see the pixie in a tablecloth sack!

'Yes, I know what you've done!' he said. 'I saw you take my needle, but I knew it would punish you, so I didn't say anything. How are you going to get out of that sack?'

'Do please help me!' begged the pixie.

'Certainly not,' said the wizard. 'You got yourself into this fix, so you must get out of it yourself too.'

'Oh, do help him, So-So,' begged all Curly-Toes' friends. 'He is very, very sorry.'

'Well, if I get you out of the sack, will you come and weed my garden every day for a week?' the wizard asked Curly-Toes.

Now the pixie hated weeding, but he couldn't do anything else but agree. So he said he would. Then So-So fetched a pair of magic scissors and – snip-snip! – the stitches were all cut and Curly-Toes was free!

Off he went home and spent the rest of the day trying to undo the stitches in his rug and curtains.

He went to bed a very sad pixie.

Then every day for a week he set off to weed the wizard's garden and, by the end of that time, he had learnt his lesson.

'I'll never, never again borrow anything without asking!' he vowed. And, as far as I know, he never did!

The Blackberry Gnome

The Blackberry Gnome

DONALD AND BESS were out blackberrying. They had a basket each, but they couldn't seem to find many berries to put into them.

'They are either unripe, or too squashy,' said Bess. 'We shall never get our basket filled at this rate.'

'We'd better go deeper into the wood,' said Donald. 'I expect most of the best ones have been picked just here.'

So they took a little path that led into the heart of the wood. They thought it was a proper path, but it wasn't. It was a rabbit path, very narrow and winding. It led the two children into a shady part of the wood, where the sunshine trickled through here and there, and lay in little pools on the bushes and grass.

'Listen!' said Bess, suddenly stopping short. 'Can you hear something?'

Donald listened. He heard a thin, clear, whistling noise coming from not far away.

'Is it a bird?' he whispered to Bess. 'I've never heard a bird that whistled quite like that before. I do wonder what kind it is.'

Both children were fond of birds, so they crept quietly forward to find out what sort it was that was singing such a sweet little song. They went down on their hands and knees, and crawled silently through the bushes, getting nearer and nearer to the whistler.

But it wasn't a bird after all! The children could hardly believe their eyes. It was the funniest little man they had ever seen. He had a little brown face with bright, bird-like eyes, and pointed ears that stuck out on each side. He was dressed in a yellow tunic, bright blue knickerbockers and long green stockings.

His hat had a blue feather in it. He wasn't even as tall as Bess.

'What is he? A brownie?' whispered Bess.

'No, a gnome, I should think,' answered Donald. 'Sh! Don't let him see us. Watch what he is doing.'

The little man was working hard, whistling his thin, sweet tune all the time. He had a big pile of baskets on the ground beside him, and he was picking blackberries from the bushes and filling the baskets at a great rate.

Bess and Donald had never seen anyone pick blackberries so fast. They could hardly see his hands, so quickly did they move. Basket after basket was filled and set neatly down in the shade. At last, when the final one was full, the gnome paused and wiped his hot forehead with an enormous yellow handkerchief.

'That's done!' he said. 'Now I really must go and get a drink. I'm so thirsty.'

The children watched him go to an old oak tree nearby. He took a key from his belt, put it into the trunk, turned it, and hey presto! A little door opened into the tree!

Bess and Donald started in astonishment. What an adventure this was! The gnome disappeared into the tree and the children heard the sound of something being poured out of a jug.

Then something strange happened. The bush just opposite the children was parted in the middle, and two or three mischievous little faces looked out.

'Come on,' said the owner of one of the faces. 'He's in his tree. It's safe for a moment!'

Out of the bush scampered about twenty tiny creatures, rather like pixies, but with little wings on their ankles and wrists instead of on their backs. Their feet made a pit-a-pat noise as they ran, like drops of rain on the ground.

Before the children could say a word, the naughty little creatures had each picked up a basket of blackberries and run off with it! Bess and Donald looked at one another.

'Well!' said Donald. 'The bad little things! Whatever will that gnome say when he finds his lovely blackberries gone?'

'We'd better tell him when he comes back,' said Bess.

'Sh! Here he comes!' said Donald.

The gnome jumped out from his tree, shut the door and locked it. Then he ran whistling to where he had left his baskets of fruit. When he saw there was none there, he stopped his whistling in dismay.

'Wh-wh-wh-what!' he cried. 'Wh-wh-wh-where have my blackberries gone? Oh dear. Oh dear! OH DEAR!'

He looked so funny that Bess and Donald, although they were sorry for him, couldn't help laughing. He heard them and came rushing round the bush behind which they sat.

'You wicked robbers!' he cried. 'You bad, naughty children! You've stolen my blackberries, and now you're laughing at me!'

Bess and Donald stopped smiling at once.

'Of course we haven't taken your blackberries!' began Donald. But the little man wouldn't take any notice of him, and stormed furiously. Then he clapped his hands loudly.

Through the trees came running half a dozen little men, just like the blackberry gnome. They ran up to him, and asked what was the matter.

'These wicked children have stolen all the blackberries that I have been growing for the fairy queen's party and only picked this morning!' cried the gnome. 'Take them away at once and lock them up!'

The gnomes took hold of Bess and Donald, and although they struggled hard, they could do nothing against the determined little men.

'Leave us alone!' cried Donald. 'I tell you we didn't take the blackberries. It was—'

'Be quiet,' said the blackberry gnome fiercely. 'What were you hiding for then? Of course you took the blackberries.'

'We didn't,' said Bess, beginning to cry. 'It was the—'

But it was no use. The gnomes wouldn't listen to a word. They dragged the two children to a big oak tree not very far away and opened a door in the side. They bundled them in, locked the door, set one of their number on guard and went off.

It was dark in the oak tree, but little by little the children made out a tiny room, with a little bed in one corner and a table in another. There were two chairs, much too small for them to sit on, so they sat on the floor.

'It's a shame!' said Donald, trying to comfort poor Bess. 'Nasty little man! Why didn't he listen to what we had to say?'

Bess wouldn't be comforted. She wept loudly. Suddenly an anxious little voice came down from above.

'Who is that crying?'

Donald peered up. Far above he could see the

daylight, for the hole in the tree went a good way up.

'Who are you?' he asked.

'I am Frisky the squirrel,' said the voice.

'What, the Frisky who lives in our garden?' cried Donald in delight.

'Yes!' said the voice in surprise. 'Why, you must be Donald and Bess! However did you come to be here?'

Quickly Donald told his story and the squirrel listened.

'It's a shame – it really is,' said Frisky. 'I shall go straight to the fairy queen herself and tell her all you say.' He disappeared, and for a long time there was silence. Then there came the sound of voices outside the tree. At last the children heard a key put into the door, and it swung open.

'Come out,' said the gruff voice of the gnome on guard.

Bess and Donald climbed out, blinking at the bright daylight. Outside was a carriage of gleaming mother-of-pearl, drawn by two swallowtail butterflies. In it sat the daintiest little person the children had ever seen. They knew her at once, for they had often seen pictures of her.

'The fairy queen!' whispered Donald to Bess. 'Frisky kept his word. He went and told her all about us!'

'Isn't she lovely,' whispered back Bess.

'These are the children I told you of,' said the voice of Frisky the squirrel, and the children saw that he was on a branch just above the queen's head.

'Tell me your story,' said the queen, gently. So Donald told her everything. By this time a little crowd of gnomes and brownies had crept round, the blackberry gnome among them, looking rather foolish.

'Why didn't you listen to the children's story before locking them up?' asked the fairy queen, turning to the blackberry gnome.

'Sorry, Your Majesty,' mumbled the gnome. 'But who were these creatures that stole the fruit, if the children didn't? That's what I should like to know!'

'I can't tell you who they were,' said Donald. 'They didn't look quite like any fairy folk I've ever seen pictures of. But their feet sounded just like drops of rain.'

'The Pit-a-Pats! The Pit-a-Pats! It must have been the Pit-a-Pats!' cried everyone. 'Oh, the naughty little things!'

'Take me to the cave of the Pit-a-Pats,' commanded the queen. 'Jump in beside me, children. And you, blackberry gnome, had better come too.'

So off they all went through the wood. Frisky the squirrel went with them, jumping from tree to tree in front of the carriage. After about fifteen minutes they came to a cave, set deep in the wood. It had a big stone in front instead of a door.

'Open, open!' cried the blackberry gnome. But it did not open. A little voice came from inside the cave.

'Ha, ha! Blackberry gnome! Is it you? You have come too late! We have eaten all your blackberries.'

'Open in the name of the queen!' cried the blackberry

gnome angrily. At once there was a frightened silence. Then the stone swung aside, and out came the same naughty little pit-a-pat creatures that the children had seen before.

They flung themselves down in front of the queen's carriage and begged for pardon. But the queen was angry and spoke sternly to them in a cold little voice.

'This is the fourth time this week you have been naughty. I shall send you to Arran the spider and he will teach you to work hard, and then you will have no time to be wicked.'

At this, a great spider came up, and threw a silver thread round the little kneeling folk. He led them all off into the wood, and the last that Bess and Donald heard of them was a loud weeping and wailing.

'I'm not sure that you don't need punishing too, blackberry gnome,' said the queen. 'You had no right to shut these children up without listening to what they had to say.'

'Please forgive him,' begged Bess. 'We don't mind

now that everything is all right, and it really was very hard to lose all his lovely blackberries as he did.'

'You're a kind little girl,' said the queen. 'I must do something to make up to you both for the unkind treatment you have had today. Would you like to come to my party tonight?'

'Ooh!' said Bess. Donald couldn't say a word. This was too good to be true.

The queen laughed.

'You shall come,' she said. 'Frisky shall show you the way home now and he will call for you at eleven o'clock tonight. Don't be late!'

Then the queen told them to get out of her carriage and follow Frisky. They thanked her very much, said goodbye, and then went after the squirrel, who was simply delighted to think that his two friends were to go to the party.

The blackberry gnome ran after them.

'Please forgive me,' he said. He looked so unhappy that Bess hugged him.

'Don't worry,' she said. 'It was worth being locked up in that nasty old tree to get an invitation from the fairy queen!'

They ran home – and you can just imagine how excited they were all the rest of the day, waiting and waiting for eleven o'clock to come!

The Whispering Pool

The Whispering Pool

ONCE UPON a time there was a boy called George who badly wanted to wish a wish that would come true. He knew what he wanted to wish – he meant to wish that he could have a hundred wishes! Then he really could have a very good time, get presents for everyone and wish everything he wanted for himself.

But somehow he could never find out how to make a wish come true. He tried all sorts of things, and wished hundreds of wishes – but they never came true.

And then one day he met Bron the brownie. He was walking down a path in Cuckoo Wood, one that he had never been down before, and he suddenly saw

Bron coming towards him. He stopped in surprise, for he knew quite well that the little man was a real, live brownie, the kind he had often seen in books.

'I say,' said George, 'I say – are you a brownie? You are, aren't you?'

'Of course,' said Bron, stopping. 'What do you want? Anything I can do to help you?'

'Oh, *yes*,' said George. 'I want to wish a wish that will come true. Can you give me a wish like that?'

'No,' said Bron. 'But I'll tell you where you can get one. You must go to the Whispering Pool in the very heart of the wood, and if you can hear what it says, and do what you are told, you can get a wish.'

'How can I?' said George, feeling very excited.

'Well, if you do what the Whispering Pool tells you and dip your hand in to drink from it at the end, you will find that whatever wish you wish will come true at once,' said Bron. 'I've often got wishes there. Look – see that path? Go straight down it, turn left by the three oak trees, turn right by the path of primroses and go on to the end. You'll find the Whispering Pool then all right.'

Off went George, feeling so excited that his knees shook. He turned left at the three oak trees, and right by the primroses, and then went straight on.

And then he came to the Whispering Pool! It was a strange place – a little brown pool set in a shallow hole in a rock. It shook and shivered and wrinkled and bubbled all the time.

'It's magic, there's no doubt about that!' said George, looking deep into it. He saw his own face looking back at him, made crooked by the ripples. He listened hard.

And he heard a bubbling whisper coming up from the strange little pool.

'Stir me as many times as there are hours in day and night! S-s-s-s-s-stir me!'

How many times did George stir the pool? He took a stick and carefully stirred the brown waters round and round, twenty-four times.

The pool bubbled tremendously and the bubbles burst with funny little pops at the surface. A green mist came from them.

It's awfully magic! thought George. *I wonder what I do next?*

A low sound came from the pool again, half a gurgle, half a whisper. 'Blow on me and spell the word "Thunder" three times!'

Gracious! thought George. *How do you spell thunder? Yes, I think I know.* So he blew on the surface of the Whispering Pool and spelt the word 'Thunder' three times.

'T-H-U-N-D-E-R!'

And when he had spelt it out three times the Whispering Pool blew up into a kind of little storm, and a low, thundery sound came from it. It was very peculiar. Then its surface calmed down, and it became so smooth that once more George could see his face there.

'What next?' said George to the pool. 'Tell me, quick!'

'Go to the oak tree and bring back the fruit it bears!' whispered the pool suddenly. 'Put it into me and stir till it is dissolved!'

The fruit of the oak tree – what's that? thought George. He ran to an oak tree and looked up at it. The tree was bare, for it was wintertime, but on it grew little round knobs of brown.

Oak apples! thought George. *That must be the fruit!* He picked one, and was just running back to the pool with it when he stopped. He remembered a nature lesson he had had that autumn about the fruits of different trees.

'The oak apple *isn't* the real fruit of the oak tree!' said George out loud. 'It's the acorn that is the fruit! Goodness, I'd have spoilt the spell if I'd dropped in this oak apple.'

He ran back to the tree and looked under it on the ground. He found an acorn, still in its cup. He was very pleased. He picked it up and ran back to the pool with it.

He dropped it in and then stirred the little brown pool till the acorn seemed to have disappeared. *I didn't know before that acorns could melt like sugar*, thought George, astonished. *This pool must be very, very magic.*

It was. It suddenly turned a bright green and sparkled brightly. A voice came out of it again, whispering like the trees in summer.

'Now dance round me seven times seven! Then drink deep!'

George felt so excited that he could hardly dance round the rock in which the strange pool lay. *Seven times seven. Now what are they?* he thought, beginning to dance solemnly round the pool. *Oh, dear, I wish I'd learnt my tables better. I'm supposed to know right up to twelve times, but I'm not at all sure of seven times. Seven sevens are – seven sevens are – oh, yes of course, they are fifty-two.*

So George carefully danced round the pool fifty-two times, counting out loud as he went. 'One ... two ... three ...'

At the number seven the pool changed to blue. At fourteen it changed to yellow. At twenty-one it changed to red and at twenty-eight it changed to purple. When George chanted thirty-five it shone golden and at forty-two it shimmered like a diamond. At forty-nine it turned to brilliant silver and shot silvery bubbles high into the air.

But when George stopped at fifty-two it had changed to its first brown colour and lay quite still. *Now*, thought George, *now to drink it! Then I'll have to wish a wish – and I'll wish for a hundred wishes – and what a time I'll have! Won't I surprise everyone?*

He dipped his curved hand into the pool, lifted the brown water to his mouth and drank. It had no taste at all. 'There!' said George. 'I've drunk from the magic pool. Now I'll wish. Well – I wish that I may have a hundred wishes and that all of them may come true!'

He stood for a moment – then he wished the first of his hundred wishes. 'I wish I was back at home!'

But nothing happened at all. George was in the

wood by the pool – he wasn't back at home. He wished the same wish again and still nothing happened. It was most disappointing.

Then he wished another wish. 'I wish a little brown pony would appear so that I might ride him home!'

But no pony appeared, though George waited patiently for ten minutes. 'Something's gone wrong,' said George very sadly. Then he wished a whole lot of different wishes, but not one of them came true.

George walked home miserably. On the way he met Bron the brownie again. 'Hallo!' said Bron. 'Did you get your wish all right?'

'No,' said George and he told him all about it, what he had done, and how careful he had been. Bron laughed.

'You were all right till the last thing you had to do,' he said. 'Seven times seven are fifty-two indeed! Why don't you learn your tables? Eight years old, aren't you – and you don't know your seven times! For shame! Now you've missed a lovely wish, for you'll never find that wishing pool again.'

'I shall look for it again and again,' said George. 'I'll find it one day – and by that time I'll know how to spell any word I'm asked, and I'll know all my tables, yes, even my thirteen times!'

But George has never found that Whispering Pool again. They say that people can only find it once – so if ever you chance to come across it, be sure you know your seven times table. *Do* you know what seven times seven are?

Millicent Mary's Surprise

Millicent Mary's Surprise

ONCE THERE was a little girl called Millicent Mary. She had a dear little garden of her own, and in the early spring the very first things to appear were the white snowdrops.

Millicent Mary loved them. She liked the straight green stalks that came up, every one holding a white bud, tightly wrapped at the top. She liked the two green leaves that sprang up each side. She loved to see the bud slowly unwrap itself and hang down like a little bell.

But she was always very disappointed because the white bells didn't ring.

'They ought to,' said Millicent Mary and she shook

each snowdrop to see if she cold make it ring. 'Bells like this should ring – they really should! Ring, little snowdrop, ring!'

But not one would ring. Still, Millicent Mary wouldn't give it up. Every morning, when she put on her hat and coat and went into the garden, she bent down and shook the snowdrops to see if perhaps today they would say *ting-a-ling-a-ling*. But they never did.

One day, she went to her garden when the snow was on the ground. The snowdrops were buried beneath it and Millicent Mary had to scrape the snow away very gently to find out where her little flowers were.

At last, all the little white bells were showing. She shook them, but no sound came. 'Well, you might have rung just a tiny tune to tell me you were grateful to me for scraping the snow away!' said Millicent Mary.

She was just going to stand up and go to the shed to fetch her broom when she saw something rather queer. The snow on the bed nearby seemed to be moving itself – poking itself up as if something was underneath it, wriggling hard.

Millicent Mary was surprised. She was even more surprised when she heard a very tiny voice crying. 'Help me! Oh, help me!'

'Goodness gracious!' said the little girl. 'There's something buried under the snow just there – and it's got a little tiny voice that speaks!'

She began to scrape away the snow and her soft, gentle fingers found something small and queer under the white blanket. She pulled out – well, guess what she pulled out!

Yes – you guessed right. It was a tiny pixie with frozen silver wings and a little shivering body dressed in a cobweb frock.

'Oh, thank you!' said the pixie in a tiny voice, like a bird cheeping. 'I was so tired last night that I crept under a dead leaf and fell asleep. And when I awoke this morning I found a great, thick, cold white blanket all over me – and I couldn't get it off! Just wait till I catch the person who threw this big blanket all over the garden!'

Millicent Mary laughed. 'It's snow!' she said. 'It isn't a real blanket. You poor little thing, you feel so cold, you are freezing my fingers. I'm going to take you indoors and get you warm.'

She tucked the pixie into her pocket and went indoors. She didn't think she would show the fairy to anyone, because she might vanish – and Millicent Mary didn't want her to do that. It was fun having a pixie, not as big as a doll, to warm before the fire!

The pixie sat on the fender and stretched out her frozen toes to the dancing flames. Millicent Mary took a piece of blue silk out of her mother's ragbag and gave it to the pixie.

'Wrap this round you for a cloak,' she said. 'It will keep out the frost when you leave me.'

The pixie was delighted. She wrapped the bit of blue silk all round her and pulled it close. 'I shall get my needle and thread and make this lovely piece of silk into a proper coat with sleeves and buttons and collar,' she said. 'You are a dear little girl! I love you. Yes, really I do. Is there anything you would like me to give *you*?'

Millicent Mary thought hard. Then she shook her head. 'No,' she said at last. 'There isn't anything at all, really. I've got all the toys I want. I did badly want a teddy bear, but I had one for Christmas. I don't want any sweets because I've got a tin of barley sugar. I don't want chocolate biscuits because Mummy bought some yesterday. No – I can't think of anything.'

The pixie looked most disappointed. 'I do wish you'd try to think of something,' she said. 'Try hard!'

Millicent Mary thought again. Then she smiled. 'Well,' she said, 'there *is* something I'd simply love – but it needs magic to do it, I think. I'd *love* it if my snowdrops could ring on my birthday, which is on 13th February!'

'Oh, that's easily managed!' said the pixie. 'I'll work a spell for it. Let me see – what's your name?'

'Millicent Mary,' said the little girl.

'"Millicent Mary",' said the pixie, writing it down in a tiny notebook. '"Birthday, 13th February. Wants snowdrops to ring on that day." All right – I'll see to it! And now goodbye, my dear. I'm deliciously warm with this blue silk. See you again some day. Don't forget to listen to your snowdrops on February 13th!'

She skipped up into the air, spread her silvery wings, and flew straight out of the top of the window. Millicent Mary couldn't help feeling tremendously excited. Her birthday would soon be there – and just imagine the snowdrops ringing!

Won't she love to shake each tiny white bell, and hear it ring *ting-a-ling-a-ling*, *ting-a-ling-a-ling!* Is *your* name Millicent Mary, by any chance, and is *your* birthday on 13th February? If it is, the snowdrops will ring for you too, without a doubt – so don't forget to shake each little white bell on that day, and hear the tinkling sound they make. What a lovely surprise for all the Millicent Marys!

A Strange Thing
to Happen

A Strange Thing
to Happen

'I'M JUST going for a run on my new roller skates, Mother!' called Julian. 'I shan't be long.'

Off he went. It was a very hot afternoon, and he thought he would skate along the lane and then turn down the path that led into the woods.

It will be cool there, he thought. *I could sit down and watch for rabbits. I might see a few.*

He skated down the path that led into the woods. Yes, it certainly was *much* cooler there!

He came to a nice little glade. Through it ran a little winding path. 'A rabbit path, I expect,' said Julian. 'I'll sit down here, behind this bush, and watch. I'll take off my skates, though.'

He took off his skates and put them carefully on one side. Then he sat down by the bush, made a little peephole through it, and began to watch the rabbit path in the glade.

But the extraordinary thing was that it didn't seem to be a rabbit path at all! It seemed to be a bus route!

The buses were really very peculiar. They were very small – as small as the toy bus that Julian had at home. They looked like motorbuses and they were filled with tiny people.

'Fairies – or pixies,' said Julian, amazed. 'And I don't believe in them! I thought you couldn't see pixies and brownies and goblins unless you believed in them – yet there they are!'

A small bus rumbled down the little winding path and disappeared in the distance. Then someone came by on a very small bicycle – a brownie with big ears and a long beard. He disappeared along the path too.

And then another bus came and it really seemed

to be going much too fast. Julian watched it. He suddenly saw a lovely little carriage coming along too, drawn by six white mice. *They'll collide!* he thought suddenly. *They can't see each other because of that sharp turn. They'll crash!*

And that is exactly what they did do. Crash! Smash! And over both bus and carriage went!

The six little mice began to squeak in fright. They couldn't run away because they were harnessed to the carriage, which was now on its side. Two of the wheels were broken. The bus was upside down and Julian could see that four of its six wheels were dreadfully bent.

What a lot of squeals and screams and shouts there were! Before he could see where they had come from, the glade was full of small people.

Goblins! Brownies – they must be brownies with those long beards, thought Julian, astonished. *Pixies – what dear little things. And what are those? Imps, perhaps, they are so small. I wonder if anyone is hurt.*

He went on peeping through the hole he had made in his bush. This was really exciting – as good as seeing a pantomime!

The little folk put the bus upright again and the carriage too. 'The wheels are broken or bent!' Julian heard them say, in little high voices like birds twittering. 'Nobody's hurt, though. What a good thing! But how are we to get the princess's carriage to her this afternoon? There are no smiths here to mend the wheels – and she wants the carriage for this evening's party.'

'And what about my bus?' called a little voice. It was the driver of the bus. 'All my passengers are going to a most important meeting. Now they won't get there.'

'We *must*!' said a brownie with his long beard blowing in the wind. 'Something must be done about it. Send for some new wheels at once.'

'Don't be silly. You can't just *send* for wheels like that,' said the driver.

It was at that very moment Julian got his idea. Wheels? Well, he had eight fine wheels he could lend them – strong ones that would carry the bus along and the carriage too. His roller skates!

He got up and went round the bush. In a trice, every single little creature disappeared. Only the bus and the carriage were left, and six frightened white mice. They stood there, trembling, because they couldn't run away.

'Hey!' called Julian, cross that everyone had gone. 'Come back! I only wanted to help you, sillies. I've got a very good idea.'

He held his skates up in his hands and jiggled them to make the wheels go round. But nobody came to see.

'All right – don't come if you don't want to,' said Julian, quite annoyed. 'I can do the mending by myself.'

He put the skates down and picked up the bus. Yes – if he pulled off the wheels, the bus body would fit quite well along one of his skates. He could tie it on with string.

He set to work. Soon he had all the bent wheels off, and the ones that were not bent too. He set the body of the little bus on the skate, and did some clever tying up with string. Ah – the bus ran well on its skate!

Then he looked at the carriage. He could take those wheels off too, and although the carriage wouldn't fit *quite* so well on a skate – it was wider and shorter – he could manage to fix it on quite nicely.

He broke off the wheels, and then set to work to fit his other skate to the underparts of the carriage. That ran beautifully too! He clicked to the little wondering mice, and they ran a few steps, pulling the queer roller skate carriage behind them – how smoothly it ran!

And then a small voice spoke just near him. 'I say – where did you get those fine wheels from?'

It was the little bus driver! He was a pixie man and he looked most admiringly at the roller skate bus.

'I'm afraid the motor of your bus is broken,' said Julian. 'But you could easily get two or three people to put ropes on the bus and pull it along on my roller skate wheels. It would run quite easily. Where's everybody gone?'

'Well – they're hiding,' said the bus driver. 'They're afraid of a giant like you. But when I saw how clever you were I just *had* to come and speak to you.'

'Tell the others to come back,' said Julian. 'I'll lend them these roller skates of mine, so that they can take the bus and the coach back safely – but I'll want my roller skates back, you know. They're new.'

'Right,' said the bus driver. He gave a loud shout. 'Come along, all of you. It's safe. This giant is friendly.'

And out poured all the little people again. Julian did indeed feel like a giant! He didn't dare to touch any of them, they looked so small and fragile.

'Isn't he clever? Is he a wizard? Did he make these big metal wheels with a spell?' asked first one and then another.

The white mice were longing to go. The coach ran so easily on its new wheels that it was no trouble at all to pull. The driver got up on his seat. He cracked a tiny whip and off they went.

Julian chuckled to see his roller skate carrying a magnificent little coach. Then off went the bus, pulled by four brownies and with the little driver in his seat.

'Don't forget I want my skates back!' called Julian, as they disappeared round a bend in the glade.

Soon the glade was quite empty again. Julian watched the winding path for a little while longer, but he saw nothing more. He thought he would go home.

'Where are your skates?' said his mother, as he came in. Julian hesitated. Should he tell what had happened? It would be rather silly, because his mother knew he didn't believe in fairies!

He did tell her, though, and she laughed. 'Oh, Julian! Fancy telling me fairy tales like that! You know you don't believe in things of that sort. You've left your skates behind. You just go and fetch them.'

But he didn't, because he knew they wouldn't be there! All the same, he did hope he would get them back.

Now, that night, when Julian was asleep, a queer noise came down the garden path. It woke him up. He knew what it was as soon as he heard it.

It was the noise made by roller skates on his garden path! He leapt out of bed and went to the window. What a peculiar sight he saw!

Each of his skates was coming down the path, driven by a small brownie. They sat on what looked like little driving seats, and held small steering wheels in their hands! One of them sounded a horn, which seemed to be on the steering wheel. Parp-parp!

The drivers got off and looked up to Julian's window. He was too astonished to do anything except wave.

The two drivers then pulled up the steering wheels, picked up their driving seats, put them over their shoulders and marched off! Well!

There were the two skates, out in the moonlight, waiting patiently to be fetched.

'I'm coming!' said Julian, and downstairs he went. He picked up the skates and saw where the steering wheel had been fixed in each – and dear me, he also saw something else!

There was a tiny motor built into each skate, so that it could drive itself along once it was set going. How wonderful!

'I'll be able to stand on my skates and turn on the little motors in them, and whizz away without even having to use my feet at all!' said Julian, pleased.

He tried it, putting on his skates and then setting off down the path. In a trice, the little motor in each skate began to purr just like the engine of a small motorbike, and away went Julian at top speed, feeling that his feet had suddenly turned into motors and were taking him away at sixty miles an hour!

He never saw the little folk again, though he went often enough to the glade and watched for hours.

He began to think he must have imagined it all.

'But it's no good thinking that,' he said to himself. 'I've got magic skates! I don't need to take a step on them – they just go by themselves. I shall be a very, very famous skater.'

So he is too. Perhaps you will see him in a roller-skating show one day and wonder how he can whizz about as he does on his shining skates. And if the name on the programme is 'Julian', well, you'll understand why he is such a marvel!

Twinkle Gets Into Mischief

Twinkle Gets Into Mischief

TWINKLE WAS a mischieveous elf if ever there was one! You wouldn't believe the things he did – all the naughtiest things his quick little mind could think of. But one day he went too far, and tried to play tricks on Snorty the dragon.

Twinkle wasn't afraid of anyone or anything, so when he heard that Snorty the dragon was looking for someone brave enough to go and paint his cave walls a nice cheerful pink, he thought he would try to get the job. So off he went, carrying a fine big pot of pink paint, whistling gaily as he skipped along.

'Hallo!' he said to Snorty, when he got to the cave.

'I hear you want your walls painted a pleasant pink.'

'Quite right,' said Snorty, blowing out some blue smoke from his nostrils.

'That's a clever trick!' said Twinkle. 'I wish I could blow smoke out of *my* nose!'

'Only dragons can do that!' said Snorty proudly. 'And look at these!'

He suddenly shot out five enormous claws from each foot – but Twinkle didn't turn a hair.

'Splendid!' he said. 'But what a business it must be for you to cut your nails, Snorty! I should think you would need a pair of shears instead of scissors!'

The dragon didn't like being laughed at. He was used to frightening people, not amusing them. So he glared at Twinkle and blew a flame out of his mouth.

'Ho, *you* don't need matches to light the gas!' chuckled Twinkle.

'That's not funny,' said Snorty sulkily. 'Get on with my painting, please, and make the walls a bright pink. And no more of your cheek, mind!'

'No more of my *tongue*, you mean!' said Twinkle, who did love having the last word. He began to mix his paint and to daub the wall with the bright pink colour. The dragon walked out in a huff and left him to it.

The cave was large and it took Twinkle all the day to do even half of it. When night came there was still half left to do. So he made up his mind to do it the next day. Snorty came back, and ate a sackful of corn for his supper. He liked the pink wall very much.

'Have you heard me roar?' he asked the elf suddenly, longing to give the cheeky little creature a real fright.

'No,' said Twinkle. 'Do roar a bit.'

So the dragon roared his loudest. Well, if you can imagine ten good thunderstorms mixed up with a thousand dustbin lids all crashing to the ground at once, and about five hundred dinner plates breaking at the same time, you can guess a little bit what the dragon's roaring was like. It was really immense.

'What do you think of that?' asked Snorty, when he had finished.

'Well,' said Twinkle, 'how do you expect me to hear you roar when you just whisper like that? I could hardly hear you!'

The dragon was so angry at this cheeky speech that he lifted Twinkle up and opened his mouth and blew smoke all over him. That made the elf angry, and he ran into a corner, very red in the face, making up his mind to play a trick on the dragon the very first chance he had!

The dragon went to bed and soon the awful sound of his snoring filled the cave. Twinkle couldn't possibly go to sleep, so he looked around for something naughty to do – and he saw the dragon's two pet geese at the end of the cave, their heads tucked under their wings. They were fine birds, as white as snow.

'Ha!' said Twinkle at once. 'I'll paint them pink. That will give old Snorty a fine shock in the morning!'

So he woke up the geese and painted the two

surprised birds a brilliant pink. They looked very strange when they were finished. Then Twinkle looked around for something else to paint. He saw the dragon's cat, a great black creature, snoozing by the fire. What fun it would be to give it a pink tail and pink whiskers!

No sooner said than done! Twinkle dipped the cat's whiskers into his paintpot and then dipped in the tail. What a dreadful sight the poor cat looked!

But that wasn't enough for Twinkle – no, he must do something even more daring than that! He would paint the dragon's beautiful brown tail! So he stole up to the snoring dragon and painted his tail a vivid pink from beginning to end. It didn't suit the dragon a bit!

Then Twinkle hid in a corner to see what the dragon would say. All the pink would easily wash off, so after the first shock, perhaps the dragon would laugh and think Twinkle was a daring elf.

But, dear me, goodness gracious, buttons and

buttercups, stars and moon! The dragon didn't think it was funny, or daring, or clever, or anything else! As soon as he woke up and saw his pink geese, his pink-tailed and pink-whiskered cat, and his own terrible pink tail, he flew into the most dreadful rage that was ever seen!

He roared so loudly that the mountain not far away had its top broken off with the shock. He blew out so much smoke that everyone for miles around wondered where the thick fog came from. He shot flames from his mouth and very nearly burnt up his cave, his geese, his cat, himself and poor, frightened Twinkle!

That silly little elf was really almost scared out of his skin. Who would have thought that Snorty would make such a fuss! Goodness gracious! Snorty roared again and blew out more smoke. Then he began to look for that naughty little Twinkle. Twinkle saw two great red eyes like engine lamps coming towards him, and he picked up his pot of paint and fled!

How he ran! How he flew! How he jumped and bounded and skipped! And after him galloped Snorty the dragon, smoke and flames flying behind him and terrible roars filling the air. Right through Fairyland they went, the two of them, for Twinkle didn't dare to stop for a minute.

At last, the elf came to the gate of Fairyland itself, and he flew over it. The dragon came up to the gate and roared to the gatekeeper to open it for him – but the pixie shook his head.

'No dragons allowed out of Fairyland,' he said.

'Very well then, I shall sit here and wait for Twinkle to come back,' roared the dragon, and down he sat, just inside the gate. And there he is still, waiting for the elf to come creeping back again.

But Twinkle is afraid to go back. So he lives in our world now, and he is really quite happy, using his paint and paintbrush all the year round. And what do you think he does? You have often seen his work, though you may not have known it. He paints the tips of the little white daisies on our lawns and in our fields! Go and look for them – you are sure to find a pretty, pink-tipped one. Then you will know that that mischievous elf Twinkle, is *somewhere* near. Call him and see if he comes!

The Fairy in the Cracker

The Fairy in the Cracker

EMMELINE WAS going to have a party. She had asked eight of her friends, and the dog next door too.

'He's always so nice to me,' she told her mother. 'I'd like him to come as well. He'll be very, very good, I know.'

'Dear me! What queer ideas you have, Emmeline!' said her mother. 'All right, ask him. Is there anyone else peculiar that you want to ask?'

'Well – I'd like to ask a fairy, if I knew one,' said Emmeline. 'But I don't. Anyway, it wouldn't be much good if I did. Do you know, Mother, not one of my friends believes in fairies? So if I *did* ask a fairy, nobody would see it but me!'

'Well, never mind – you don't know one so you can't send an invitation,' said Mother, laughing.

Now, that night was very very cold, and the frost was hard and bitter out of doors. A small fairy called Little-Wings couldn't keep herself warm. She had a spiderweb cloak, which didn't keep out the wind, and her hiding place was a mossy hole in a bank, into which the wind blew all night.

'I *must* get warm. I must, I must!' said Little-Wings, shivering so much that she could hardly stand up. She crept out of her hole and flew to the house nearby. It was the one where Emmeline lived. A window was open at the top, and Little-Wings just managed to squeeze in nicely. She found herself in a big sitting room in which a fire was just dying down. The room was dark except for the embers of the fire, glowing red. Little-Wings flew down to warm herself. Oh, how lovely! She sat on the warm rug and held out her tiny hands to the fire.

And then somebody came running up, squeaking crossly. 'Get away! Who are you? Have you come to find the crumbs on the floor? I won't have it. Get away!'

It was a small, grey-brown mouse with long whiskers. Little-Wings was very frightened because she was much smaller than the mouse. He seemed very fierce indeed to her.

'I won't eat your crumbs,' she said. 'I don't want them.'

'Now, you just go away,' said the mouse, 'else I might eat *you*! I don't want you here. This is *my* home, not yours. My hole is in the corner over there and when everyone has gone to bed this is *my* playground! Go away!'

'Oh, just let me warm my toes!' begged Little-Wings, but the mouse wouldn't. He rushed at her and knocked her over. In fright, she spread her wings and flew into the air. But wherever she alighted that mouse watched for her, and ran at her. When she flew on to the table he even ran up the cloth and almost knocked her off the edge of the table!

Little-Wings saw a box on the table. She ran to it, tilted up the cardboard lid and slipped inside. But the mouse followed her! Little-Wings found that the box was full of long, papery things. She didn't know they were crackers, put ready for the party next day. She scrambled into the end of one of them, and squeezed her tiny body right into the very middle of the cracker.

The mouse couldn't follow her. He was too big. He squeaked angrily at her. 'All right, all right! You stay there and don't dare to come down and eat my crumbs. You stay there!'

So Little-Wings stayed in the very middle of the cracker, sitting beside a red cap and a tiny brooch, which were what would pop out when the cracker was pulled. It was quite warm there. Little-Wings grew sleepy. She curled herself up inside the cracker and fell fast asleep.

And in the morning she didn't dare to creep out of

the cracker, because the room was full of voices! Mother was there and Emmeline, and Auntie Hetty and Cousin John – all making ready for the party!

'I hope we'll have enough crackers,' said Auntie, opening the box where Little-Wings was hiding in one of them. 'My word – these look beauties! I'm longing to pull one and hear it go BANG!'

Well, three o'clock came, and all the eight visitors trooped in, looking beautiful in their party clothes. Bonzo the dog next door arrived too, wearing a grand red bow and on his very best behaviour. He had told every dog in the street about the party, and how they envied him!

It was a lovely party, with a perfectly marvellous tea. And then suddenly Little-Wings felt the box of crackers lifted high in the air! Somebody put in a hand and began to take the crackers out one by one, and give them to each child.

Little-Wings was given to Emmeline! She sat inside the cracker, shivering with fright. *Now* what was going to happen to her? She didn't know she was inside a cracker that was meant to be pulled. She had never seen a cracker before in her life!

'Pull my cracker with me, Katy, pull it!' cried Emmeline excitedly, and she held it out to Katy.

Katy took the other end, and the two little girls pulled hard. BANG! The cracker went off beautifully and out of it came the paper cap, the little brooch and Little-Wings herself, flying high on silvery wings, frightened and trembling!

'Look! Look! A fairy!' squealed Emmeline in astonishment. 'Look, everybody, look! There was a fairy in my cracker. She's come to my party. Look!'

'Where? Where? Don't be silly, Emmeline! There isn't a fairy!' cried all her friends. You see, they didn't believe in fairies, so they couldn't see Little-Wings at all. But somebody else saw her – and that somebody was Bonzo, the dog. *He* saw her quite plainly and followed her with his eyes as she flew to the top of the window.

'Woof,' he said to Emmeline, which meant, 'I saw her too!'

Emmeline ran to the window, but Little-Wings was gone – gone out into the cold night again. Poor Little-Wings, what a fright she had had when the cracker went BANG just beside her!

'Mother! Did you see the fairy? Didn't *anyone* see her?' cried Emmeline. But no – nobody had. Nobody except Bonzo. So the party went on.

You'll want to know where Little-Wings went to. Well, she flew down to a small wooden house, which smelt warm and cosy, with straw piled into it. It was Bonzo's kennel – and when he got home from the party, and snuggled into his kennel, there was Little-Wings.

He licked her tiny hand. 'Don't be afraid,' he wuffed, gently. 'I saw you at the party. You should have stayed. It was such fun. How tiny you are! Would you like to stay with me in my kennel?'

So that's where Little-Wings is living while the

cold weather lasts. She is getting over the shock of being pulled in a cracker and will soon forget it.

But Emmeline has never forgotten. She doesn't care what the others say – she *knows* there was a fairy at her party.

The Storm Fairies
Get Into Mischief

The Storm Fairies
Get Into Mischief

ONCE UPON a time the storm fairies decided to have the grandest picnic that had ever been held.

'Queen Titania of the wood fairies is always holding dances and King Neptune down in the sea has swimming sports,' they said. 'Why shouldn't we have something grand too? People don't think enough of us – we'll make them take notice of us for a change!'

So they planned a wonderful picnic.

'We'll have it up in the clouds,' they decided. 'We'll choose a fine black one, then our silver and glass will look lovely against it. And we'll put hailstones in the lemonade to make it icy cool, and we'll mix snow with our sugar to make it white and frothy. Oh, we'll have a *beautiful* picnic!'

Now, the storm fairies are very boastful. If they want to tell a piece of news to the world they make the thunder shout it out for them, and if they want to light a candle they use a flash of lightning to do it with, just to show everyone how clever they are.

So they weren't very much liked. Nobody was quite certain how far they could be trusted. King Neptune especially disliked them, for they had a bad habit of asking the North Wind to blow just as he was taking a nice quiet sail on his favourite jellyfish. They liked to see him tumble off, but *he* didn't like it at all. He said it hurt his dignity, and that is much more painful than you'd think.

Well, the invitations were soon sent out. The storm fairies got the South Wind to take them, and a very useful little messenger he was. He simply took a look at the address on an envelope, blew it in the right direction, and off it went floating to the doorstep of the one invited. It was different for the sea sprites, of course. The South Wind had to blow the letter on to the wave above their house, and the sea sprites came up and fetched it quickly.

Soon all the invitations were delivered, and the storm fairies sat down on a silvery cloud and waited for the answers. But for a long time none came.

Everyone was wondering what to do. They couldn't make up their minds whether to go or not.

'Those storm fairies are so queer,' said the Lord High Chamberlain of Fairyland. 'They're what I call blow-hot, blow-cold people. You never know if they're going to smile at you sweetly in the sunshine, or shout at you in a snowstorm. For myself, Your Majesty, I prefer not to go. Last time I met one he put three hailstones down my back just because I didn't admire his new hat.'

'Yes, and I remember once when we were all admiring a lovely mauve cloud,' said the queen, 'the storm fairies opened it in the middle and drenched us with water. I think, on the whole, we won't go. It would be just like them to let the cloud we were sitting on suddenly dissolve into rain and let us fall if we didn't like their wonderful picnic. Send answer to say we cannot come.'

King Neptune and the sea sprites were deciding much the same thing. His Lord Chancellor was very anxious to refuse all the invitations in case something awkward happened.

'Don't you remember that day you told them they were boastful?' he said. 'They sent you a present the day after, and when you opened it at breakfast time you found it was a little hailstorm. A horrible thing to have at the breakfast table. It quite spoilt the taste of your marmalade, you said.'

'Yes, I remember,' said Neptune thoughtfully. 'I remember a good many things like that, in fact. There was one time when they met you out, and lit your pipe for you with a lightning flash; do you remember that? I've never seen you fall over quite so quickly before.'

'These things are best forgotten,' said the chancellor hastily. 'Shall we refuse the invitation or not?'

'Yes, refuse them,' said Neptune. 'I'll arrange something with Titania and the fairies for that day, so that the storm fairies will think we couldn't go owing to a – what do you call it, chancellor? Oh, yes, a previous engagement.'

So everyone sent to say that they couldn't go to the picnic. The storm fairies were furious.

'It's not often we do anything really nice,' said one honestly, 'and *this* is what happens when we do! *Why* can't everyone come?'

'I'll go and see,' said another and flew straight off.

He flew down to the shore, and there saw the Lord High Chamberlain of Fairyland and the Lord Chancellor of the sea talking together. He hid behind a rock and heard what they were saying. They were arranging to have some beach sports between the fairies and the sea sprites, and they were to be held on the same day as the storm fairies had hoped to hold their picnic. Off flew the storm fairy in a terrible temper to tell the others what he had heard.

'All right!' said all the others. 'We'll just spoil their sports. Now how can we do it?'

'I know!' cried one. 'What about going to Neptune's stables and letting out all the white horses he's so proud of? There won't be anyone watching them on that day!'

'Yes, that's a fine idea!' cried the storm fairies. 'We'll jump on their backs and ride them straight up to the beach, and upset all the sports! What fun it will be!'

The scamps waited impatiently for the day to come. At last, when it came, they slid down a convenient rainbow and dropped into the sea just near the stables. In these were kept the beautiful white horses belonging to King Neptune. He was very proud of them and used them whenever there was a procession. They had wonderfully curly white manes and long white tails.

The stables were unguarded. Everyone had gone to

the sports on the beach. The doors were bolted on the outside, and it was only the work of a moment to slip all the bolts undone and scramble into the stables.

Suddenly, with a tremendous neighing, the biggest horse rushed out of his stable with a small storm fairy sitting tightly on his back, clinging to his mane. All the others followed.

The storm fairies turned the horses' heads to the shore and began galloping for all they were worth.

'Now we'll upset things!' they shouted.

But they made such a noise that Neptune and Titania heard it, and jumped to their feet in wonder. And there, far away out at sea, they saw the curly white manes of the horses flashing out here and there as they galloped along under the water.

'The white horses are out!' shouted Neptune. 'What *shall* we do? They'll rush out of the water on to the land and scare everyone into a fit! Oh, what *shall* we do?'

The horses were coming nearer and nearer.

'Quick!' cried Titania. 'Think of a sea-spell to keep them in the water, Neptune!'

Neptune thought hard and then drew a circle quickly in the sand. He stepped inside, pointed to the sea, and chanted a magic spell to stop the horses galloping out.

They were so near that their neighing could be heard. Nearer and nearer they came, and nearer and nearer.

'They're coming out!' screamed the fairies and sprites and hid themselves behind the rocks.

But just as the water's edge was nearly reached – SPLASH-CRASH-SPLASH! Over went the horses, tumbling in the spray, and then they quickly turned and went galloping off to the sea again.

And all the storm fairies were thrown off into the water and rolled higgledy-piggledy everywhere, right up to Neptune's feet.

'It's the storm fairies who have let the white horses out!' he cried in astonishment. 'Look at them!'

Everyone came running to look. The storm fairies

were so surprised and so startled at their fall that they let every wave bundle them over and box their ears and splash in their faces.

'Just wait till they get out and we'll give them such a spanking!' cried the chancellor, remembering the many shocks he had had.

But the white horses were never caught again. They became so wild that no one dared to touch them. They roam all about the sea, and when the storm fairies are anywhere about the white horses run away in terror, and try to get on to the land again. But they can't, because of Neptune's magic spell.

Watch for them at the seaside on the next stormy day. You will spy their curly white manes far out at sea, and you will see them come nearer and nearer and nearer – till splash, the magic spell gets them, and they tumble in the foam and race back into the deep green ocean once again!

Fiddle-De-Dee's Spell

Fiddle-De-Dee's Spell

FIDDLE-DE-DEE AND TWINKLES both went to the same brownie school. They were the greatest of friends and they always played games together and sat next to each other when they were in class.

But one day they quarrelled. It was a dreadful quarrel, and they both called each other some very rude brownie names. It was all because of an apple.

Fiddle-De-Dee had brought a lovely apple to school for his mid-morning break, and Twinkles had brought a big shiny bun. Each brownie liked the look of what the other had, so they decided to share what they had brought between them. Twinkles was going to give Fiddle-De-Dee half of his bun and in return he would have half of Fiddle-De-Dee's apple.

So at eleven o'clock, when their teacher sent all the brownies out to play, Twinkles cut his big shiny bun exactly in half and the two ate it. It was absolutely delicious.

Then Fiddle-De-Dee took out his knife and sliced his apple in half. One half he gave to Twinkles and the other half he kept to himself.

But when Twinkles bit into his half, what should he find but a large grub, and he could not eat any of his piece at all! Fiddle-De-Dee saw the grub too and he quickly crammed all his piece of apple into his mouth before Twinkles had a chance to ask him for a bit.

'That's not fair!' cried Twinkles in a rage. 'I gave you half my bun and it was all perfectly good, and now you've gobbled up the good half of your apple without even offering me a small piece of it! I say that you are a mean, greedy brownie, Fiddle-De-Dee!'

Then they began to have a very big quarrel indeed,

and all the other brownies came round and listened in surprise, for everyone knew what good friends the two brownies usually were.

Twinkles knew far more horrible names than Fiddle-De-Dee knew, and Fiddle-De-Dee got crosser and crosser. At last he clapped his hands twice and shouted, 'If you say any more, I'll put a nasty spell on you!'

'You don't know any, you poor, twisty-toed little tiddlywinks!' shouted back Twinkles.

'Oh yes I do!' shouted Fiddle-De-Dee. 'I know an excellent spell for stupid people with hardly any brains, like you! I can use a spell to make your silly little head half as small as it already is. Then what will you look like? Everyone will point their fingers and laugh at you! Ho, ho, that really would be a fine spell to put on you, Twinkles!'

Twinkles began to feel uncomfortable. Fiddle-De-Dee looked so fierce. Suppose – just suppose he really did know a spell like that! What a dreadful thing it would be to go home with his head made half as small again! Whatever would his mother say?

Just then the school bell rang to let all the brownies know that it was time to go back into their classroom again, and off they all ran. Twinkles felt upset and could hardly do any work. He sat and moped, sometimes looking at Fiddle-De-Dee, who made dreadful faces at him whenever he could.

After school was over Twinkles rushed to the cloakroom before anyone else. He didn't want to wait for Fiddle-De-Dee. He really did feel quite frightened of him. He snatched down a hat from its peg, crammed it on his head and ran off home.

After he had run a little way he felt out of breath, so he slowed down. His hat fell forward on to his nose with a plop. Twinkles pushed it back impatiently. It slid forward again, right over his eyes, so that he couldn't see.

Two pixies who were passing by began to laugh. They pointed their fingers at Twinkles and shouted,

'Grow a larger head, little brownie, grow a larger head! Then your hat might just manage to stay on it!'

When he heard the pixies' shouts Twinkles grew pale. Grow a larger head! Oh, goodness gracious, was his head growing smaller? Had Fiddle-De-Dee put that horrible spell on him after all? His hat slid forward once again and rested on his nose.

'He's made my head small, just like he said he would!' wailed poor Twinkles in despair. 'Oh, what a terrible sight I shall look! What will my mother say? How can I go to school this afternoon? Everyone will point their fingers and laugh at me!'

Crying loudly, he ran home, and his mother was astonished to see her little brownie son come indoors with his hat on his nose and his mouth wide open, crying for all he was worth. In a minute or two Twinkles told her all that had happened.

His mother was very angry indeed. She took Twinkles' hand and marched him off to Fiddle-De-Dee's home. Fiddle-De-Dee was just going in at his gate. He turned round when he saw Twinkles and his mother. When he saw how angry Mrs Twinkles looked, he was frightened and ran indoors and hid. Into the house marched Twinkles' mother, dragging her brownie son by the hand, for he could not see to walk with his hat on his nose. Fiddle-De-Dee's mother came to see what was the matter, and she stared at Twinkles in amazement.

'Where is that wicked son of yours?' cried Twinkles' mother. 'See what he has done to my poor little boy. He has put a spell on him to make his head small, and now his hat slips down on his nose all the time!'

'But – but – surely Fiddle-De-Dee wouldn't do a thing like that!' said Mrs Fiddle-De-Dee in surprise. 'They are such great friends. Fiddle-De-Dee! Fiddle-De-Dee! Where are you?'

Fiddle-De-Dee crept out from under the table. He was very frightened. His mother took hold of him and asked, 'Is it true that you have put a spell on your friend Twinkles to make his head grow small?'

'No, oh, no!' said Fiddle-De-Dee, beginning to cry. 'I don't know a spell like that! I only said I did, just to frighten Twinkles. I don't know why his head's gone small, indeed I don't. We did quarrel this morning, but I wouldn't really hurt him for anything in the world!'

Mrs Fiddle-De-Dee took off Twinkles' hat to have a good look at his head. She looked at it and looked at it. Then she turned to Mrs Twinkles.

'His head doesn't really seem any smaller to me,' she said. 'It seems about the same size as usual.'

Mrs Twinkles looked at her brownie son's head, and then she looked again. 'You are right,' she said. 'It really doesn't look any smaller than it was. How odd! How is it that his hat is slipping down over his nose then, and doesn't fit him as it usually does? That is certainly very strange.'

Then Fiddle-De-Dee came forward, a sudden idea in his mind. He picked up the hat, which had been put down on the table and he had a look inside it.

Then he gave a shout.

'Look!' he said. 'Twinkles has got the wrong hat! This hat belongs to Heyho Brownie, whose head is the biggest in the whole school. It wouldn't fit anyone else at all, and it isn't any wonder it kept slipping down on to Twinkles' nose! Oh dear, oh dear, how very funny!'

Twinkles stared at Fiddle-De-Dee. So his head hadn't gone small after all! It was only that he had taken the wrong hat – one that was much, much too large for him!

Mrs Twinkles looked at Mrs Fiddle-De-Dee and they both began to smile – and, before anyone could say another word, all four brownies burst out laughing, holding their sides, and rolling about the room, chuckling and giggling for all they were worth!

Well, of course, you have to be friends when you all laugh together like that, and when they had finished, Twinkles and Fiddle-De-Dee hugged one another, and Mrs Twinkles and Mrs Fiddle-De-Dee kissed each other on the cheek. Then, still smiling, they said goodbye, and Twinkles and his mother went happily off to lunch.

And that was the end of the quarrel, except that Heyho Brownie was very angry indeed with Twinkles for taking his hat home by mistake.

'What do you suppose I looked like with your silly little hat perched on top of my head?' he shouted to Twinkles that afternoon. 'I've a good mind to punish you!'

But Fiddle-De-Dee came to Twinkles' help. 'Leave my friend Twinkles alone!' he said – and he looked so fierce that Heyho Brownie crept away, feeling rather frightened.

'It's so nice to be friends again,' said Twinkles happily. 'Don't let's ever quarrel again, Fiddle-De-Dee!'

And they never, ever did!

Peronel's Magic Polish

Peronel's Magic Polish

ONCE UPON a time there was a little fairy called Peronel. He lived in the king of Fairyland's palace, and his work was to clean all the brass that the head footman brought into the kitchen.

He was very good at this. He would sit all morning, and rub and polish away till the brass fire irons and trays shone beautifully.

'That's very nice, Peronel,' the cook would say to him every morning.

This made him very happy and he beamed with pride. He thought that no one had ever polished brass as beautifully as he did.

One day, as Peronel sat polishing a brass coal bucket, he had a great idea.

'I know what I'll do!' he said. 'I'll invent a new polish that will make everything twice as dazzling as before! I think I know just where to find the right ingredients. How delighted everyone will be!'

So that night he slipped out into the woods and gathered roots and leaves, and a magic flower that only blossomed at midnight, and two cobwebs just newly made. Then he went back to bed.

Next day he boiled everything together, strained it through the cook's sieve and left it to cool. Then he went to the Wizened Witch, and asked her to sell him a little pot with a brightness spell inside. She told him, 'Empty this into your mixture at sunset, stir it well and sing these words:

'*Now the magic has begun,*
Polish brighter than the sun!

'Then everything you polish will be brighter than it ever was before!'

'Oh, thank you!' cried Peronel, and ran happily off clutching the little pot, after paying the Wizened Witch a bright new penny he had polished the day before.

When the sun sank slowly down in the sky, Peronel fetched his jar of polish. He emptied the witch's spell of brightness into it, stirred it, and sang:

'Now the magic has begun,
Polish brighter than the sun!'

Next morning Peronel proudly put the polish he had made on the kitchen table, and started work. He had six brass candlesticks to clean and a table lamp. He worked very hard indeed for a whole hour until the cook came into the kitchen. She stopped and threw up her hands in great surprise.

'My goodness, Peronel!' she cried in astonishment.

'What have you been doing to those candlesticks! I can hardly look at them, they're so bright!'

'I'm using a magic polish, you see,' said Peronel proudly. 'Isn't it lovely! I made it all myself!'

The cook called the footmen and the ladies' maids and the butler, to see what a wonderful job Peronel had done.

'Look how bright Peronel has made the candlesticks!' she said. 'Isn't he clever? He's made up a magic polish of his own!'

Everybody thought Peronel was certainly very clever indeed, and the little fairy was delighted. But he longed to do something that would make the king and queen notice him too.

You'd never guess what he did!

He fetched the king's golden crown in the middle of the night, and gave it a tremendous polishing with his magic polish! Then he quietly put it back again.

In the morning the king couldn't make out what had happened to his gleaming crown.

'It's so bright I can't bear to look at it,' he said to the queen. 'It shines like the sun!'

'Put it on, then your eyes won't be dazzled,' said the queen, and the king took her advice.

But Peronel's polishing had not only made the crown bright, it had made it terribly slippery too, and it wouldn't stay straight. It kept slipping, first over one ear, then over the other, and everybody in court began to giggle.

The king became quite cross.

'Well, I don't know who's been polishing my crown,' he said, 'but, anyway, I wish they wouldn't! It's a silly idea!'

Peronel was just nearby and heard what the king said. Instead of being a sensible little fairy and deciding not to try to make people praise him any more, he became quite angry.

All right, he thought. *I'll polish something else tonight! Nobody will know who's done it and I'll have a bit of fun!*

So the naughty little fairy took his polish and his

cloth into the king's breakfast room that night, and began polishing the gold chairs with all his might.

You can imagine what happened next morning! The king and queen, the princess and the prince, all sat down to breakfast, but they couldn't sit still! They slid and slipped and slithered about on their chairs, till the footmen standing behind nearly burst themselves with trying not to laugh!

When the king disappeared under the table, everybody thought it was very funny – even the queen.

'Dear, dear, dear!' she said, laughing. 'I never saw you disappear so quickly before! I really think we'd better sit on some other chairs until the polish has worn off! Goodness knows who has made them so shiny and slippery!'

'I'll soon find out!' said the king crossly, looking very red in the face as he sat down on another chair.

'No, no, dear,' said the queen. 'It was only an accident! Somebody's been doing his work too well!'

When Peronel heard what had happened, he was

very pleased and chuckled loudly. He wished he had seen it all.

I'd like to polish something and see what happens myself, he thought. *Now, what can I polish? I know! There's a dance tomorrow night in the ballroom. I'll ask if I can help to polish the floor, and then I'll hide behind a curtain and watch all the people slipping about!*

The naughty little fairy found it was quite easy to get permission to help. The other servants were only too glad to have him, for they all knew how quick and clever he was.

While they were at lunch, he mixed a little of his magic polish into all their pots, and then ran in to his own lunch.

All afternoon Peronel and the other servants polished the floor in preparation for the dance, until it shone like sunlight.

'Dear me!' said the butler, peeping in. 'You have all worked well!'

He came into the big room – and suddenly his legs

slid from beneath him and he sat down on the floor with a bump.

'Good gracious!' he cried. 'Isn't the floor slippery!'

Peronel chuckled. Then he darted behind a curtain, waiting for the evening, when the guests would come in and dance.

At last they came, chattering and laughing. But directly they began to dance on the slippery floor, their feet didn't seem to belong to them! They went slithering everywhere – then bumpity-bump, the guests began tumbling down, as if they were dancing on ice!

Just then the king came into the ballroom, and stared in the greatest astonishment. Half the dancers were on the floor! 'What is the matter?' he cried, striding forward.

He soon knew – for his feet flew from under him and – bump! – he sat down suddenly.

'Who has polished the floor like this?' he thundered. 'It's as slippery as ice. Fetch the servants. I shall punish them!'

Peronel trembled behind the curtain and wondered what he should do. He wasn't a coward, and he knew he couldn't let the servants be punished for something that was his fault.

So, to the king's surprise, Peronel rushed out from behind the curtain and ran up to where His Majesty still sat on the floor. But he forgot that it was slippery, and he suddenly slipped, turned head-over-heels and landed right in the king's lap!

'Bless my buttons!' roared the king in fright. 'Whatever's happened now?'

Very frightened indeed, Peronel got up off the king's lap and stood trembling as he confessed what he had done.

'It wasn't the other servants' fault; it was mine,' he said. 'And it was I who polished your crown the other day, but I only meant to be useful, truly I did!'

'You're a great deal too useful,' the king said crossly, getting up very carefully. 'You can choose your own punishment, Peronel. You can either stay in the palace and never polish anything again, or leave the palace and take your wonderful polish with you.'

Sadly, Peronel wondered what to do.

'I don't want to do anything else but polish,' he said at last. 'So I'm afraid I'll have to leave the palace and take my magic polish with me.'

And he did, and what do you suppose he does with it now?

He goes to the fields and meadows and polishes every single golden yellow buttercup that he finds. Look inside one and you'll see how beautifully he does it! He misses his friends at the palace, but now he has made new friends with all the little creatures of the countryside, and he spends his days happily polishing to his heart's content!

The Wrong Side
of the Bed

The Wrong Side
of the Bed

LONG, LONG ago, the wizard Ten-Toes bought a marvellous bed. There were dragons carved at the head, with long, coiling bodies, and peacocks with spreading tails carved at the foot. The dragons had eyes of rubies and the peacocks had eyes of sapphire blue, so you can guess how strange they looked with their eyes gleaming in the dark at night. The wizard liked the bed very much. He said it made him feel more like a wizard than ever.

He had bought it from a witch, and when she sold it to him she said, 'Ten-Toes, whatever you do, always get out on the *right* side of the bed. If you don't, you'll be sorry!

She wouldn't tell him why, but she knew quite well. A bad-tempered little imp had made the bed for himself. One day the witch had placed a spell upon him, got him into her power and taken the bed for her own. But she could not get rid of the little imp. He made himself invisible and squatted down beside his beautiful bed, which he would not leave night or day. The witch found it out one morning by getting out on the side of the bed where the imp crouched.

What a shock for her! He bit her foot and his sharp teeth sent poison into her – the poison of his own bad temper. And that day the witch couldn't do anything right! How she scolded, how she raged! How she stamped her foot and frowned! It was terrible to see.

She sold Ten-Toes the bed, but she wouldn't say a word about the invisible imp that went with it, for she was afraid that if she did he would not pay her so much money. The wizard was pleased with the bed.

He slept well in it and was careful each morning to get out on the right side.

One day he forgot. He was sleepy and got out the wrong side. He trod on the invisible imp, who at once bit him in a rage. 'Dear, dear!' said the wizard, surprised. 'I must have stepped on a pin!'

All that day things went wrong for Ten-Toes. He lost his temper, he shouted and raged. He hit the man who came to clean the windows, he shook his fist at the woman who sold him potatoes. Really, he behaved very badly indeed. The bad-temper poison was working very strongly in him!

The next morning Ten-Toes got out the *right* side of the bed and things went well. The morning after he got out the *wrong* side, and everything went wrong again because of his bad temper. He simply couldn't understand it!

He met the witch and frowned at her so fiercely that she was frightened and astonished. Then she suddenly thought of something.

'Did you get out of bed the wrong side this morning?' she called after him. The wizard stopped and thought. Yes, he had! Dear, dear, dear! So that explained his bad temper, did it? What a peculiar thing! Well, he would be careful to get out the *right* side after that!

That was hundreds of years ago! But it's a strange thing, isn't it, that we still say to a bad-tempered person, 'You must have got out of bed on the wrong side this morning!' Now you know how that saying began!

The Talking Shoes

The Talking Shoes

ONCE THERE was a little girl called Jennifer. She walked a mile to school each day and back, and that was quite a long way. Sometimes it rained and then she took her mackintosh. Sometimes it was cold and she took her coat – and sometimes it was very hot and she wore no coat at all, but a shady hat in case she got sunstroke.

One day she set out in the sunshine. It was a nice, sunny, autumn day. Jennifer had a short coat on and her lace shoes and her school hat. She ran along, singing a song she was learning at school.

Halfway to school, a great black cloud came

up and it began to pour with rain. How it poured! You should have seen it. The rain came down like slanting lines of silver, and big puddles came all along the road.

Jennifer stood under a tree to shelter herself. When the rain stopped she ran out into the road again – and stepped right into a most enormous puddle! It was deeper than her ankles – so she wetted her shoes and socks dreadfully.

'Goodness gracious!' said Jennifer in dismay. 'Now look what I've done! I shall have to sit in school with wet shoes and socks all morning and I shall get an awful cold.'

She walked along very sadly, thinking of how she would sneeze and cough the next day – and then she passed by a little yellow cottage where a dear old lady lived all alone. The old lady was shaking the crumbs off her tablecloth for the birds in the garden, and she called to Jennifer. 'Did you get caught in that rainstorm, my dear?'

'Yes, I did,' said Jennifer sadly. 'And just look at my shoes and socks! I stepped into a puddle and they are wet through!'

'Dear me, that's very dangerous,' said the old woman at once. 'Come along in and I'll see if I can lend you a pair of my stockings and a dry pair of shoes. I have a very small foot, so maybe I can manage something for you.'

So Jennifer went into the tidy little cottage, and the old lady found a pair of lace shoes for Jennifer, and a pair of brown stockings.

'There!' she said. 'These will do nicely. I can lend you a pair of garters too, to keep up the stockings. Put them on, my dear, and I will dry your wet things and have them ready for you by the time you pass by at dinner time.'

Jennifer put on the stockings. Then she put on the shoes. They had big tongues to them and long laces, but they were most comfortable. They felt nice and dry too.

'Thank you,' said Jennifer gratefully. 'I'll try not to tread in any more puddles with these on.'

She skipped off to school. The old lady stood at the gate and called after her. 'Oh – Jennifer dear – just a minute. Don't be naughty at school today, will you? You may be sorry if you are!'

How funny! thought Jennifer. *Why should I have to be specially good today?* I *don't know!*

Jennifer was not very good at school. She whispered and talked when she shouldn't. She smudged and blotted her writing book instead of keeping it nice and tidy. She pulled the plaits of the little girl in front and she pinched the boy next to her because she didn't like him. So you see she really wasn't a very good child at school.

She didn't see any real reason why she should be good that day. So she didn't try. She took her place in her classroom and got out her books. She took up her number book so roughly that a page tore in half.

Then a funny thing happened. A voice spoke in the

silence of the classroom – a rather deep-down, husky voice that no one had ever heard before.

'Careless girl, isn't she?' said the voice. 'Did you see how she tore her number book?'

'Yes, I did,' said another voice, just as deep-down and husky. 'She ought to lose a mark for that.'

'Who is talking?' asked Miss Brown in astonishment, looking round the class. The voices didn't sound a bit like any of the girls' voices. The children stared round in amazement. Jennifer went red. How dared somebody talk about her like that?

She wondered if it was the little boy next to her. She pinched him slyly. A voice spoke loudly again.

'Did you see Jennifer pinch the little boy next to her? Isn't she cruel?'

'A most unkind child,' said the second voice. 'I don't think I like her.'

'Oh! Who's talking like that about me!' cried Jennifer in a rage.

'It sounds like somebody on the ground,' said

Miss Brown, puzzled and alarmed. Everyone looked on the floor. Nobody was hiding beneath the tables or desks.

Have you guessed what it was that was talking? Perhaps you have! It was the tongues in the two borrowed shoes! They chatted away to one another, and were most surprising to hear.

'I think she has a very cross face, don't you?' asked one tongue. 'It's a pity she doesn't look in the glass. Then she would see how horrid she looks when she keeps frowning.'

'Will you stop talking, whoever it is?' cried Miss Brown, and she rapped on her desk.

The shoes held their tongues and stopped talking for a while. They were frightened of Miss Brown. The class settled down to write. They were copying from the blackboard. Jennifer did not try very hard. When she opened her desk to get out some blotting paper her book slid to the floor.

'Good gracious!' said one tongue to the other. 'Just

look at Jennifer's dreadful writing! Did you ever see anything so awful for a child of ten? Really, she ought to be ashamed of herself.'

'Poor thing! Perhaps she is a stupid child and can't write any better,' said the other tongue, flapping itself a little. 'Look at that blot – and three smudges on one page! If I were the teacher I would put Jennifer into the corner!'

'Oh! Oh!' cried Jennifer, stamping her foot and bursting into tears. 'I won't stand it! Who is saying these horrid things about me?'

'I can't imagine, Jenny,' said Miss Brown. 'All I can say is that the things are perfectly true! It is a shocking thing that a girl of ten should write so badly and be so untidy.'

Jennifer picked up her book sulkily and put it on her desk. The shoes chatted together again.

'She's got her horrid sulky face on now. Isn't she a most unpleasant child? I wonder how many smudges she will make on her next page!'

Jennifer set her teeth and made up her mind to make no smudges at all. She wrote a really beautiful page and showed it to Miss Brown.

'Good gracious, Jennifer! I've never seen such nice writing from you before!' cried Miss Brown.

'You see, she *can* do it if she tries,' said one shoe. 'She's just too lazy to do it always.'

'I'm not lazy, I'm not lazy!' cried Jennifer, and she stamped her foot. That gave the shoes such a shock that they said nothing at all for a whole hour. Then it was geography, a lesson that Jennifer didn't like. She leant over and pulled the plaits of the little girl in front of her. The little girl squealed.

'Somebody pulled my hair!' she cried. Miss Brown looked up crossly.

'Was it you, Jenny?' she asked.

'No, Miss Brown,' said Jennifer untruthfully.

'OoooooooOOOOOH!' said one shoe to the other. 'Isn't she untruthful? Really! Oooooooh!'

'Untruthful, cowardly and unkind,' said the other

shoe. 'Why doesn't somebody smack her and send her to bed?'

Jennifer glared round at everyone, thinking that *somebody* must be playing a trick on her, talking like this. But everyone was as astonished as she was.

'Who *is* talking!' cried Miss Brown, quite alarmed again. 'I don't like this. I shall put the talkers into the corner if I hear any more.'

'Fancy! She'd put us in the corner!' giggled a shoe. 'Well, she'd have to put Jenny there too, if she put us.'

'Perhaps we'd better not talk,' said the other shoe. 'I believe we are disturbing the class a little. Sh!'

So they said no more until it was time to go home. Then Jennifer went sulkily to the cloakroom and took down her hat and coat. Another child got in her way, and she gave him a push that sent him right over.

'Isn't she rough?' said a shoe, shocked. 'Did you see her push that nice little boy right over? If she did that to me, I'd kick her!'

'And I'd trip her up!' said the other shoe fiercely.

'Horrid girl! Do you suppose anyone in the world likes her at all?'

'I expect her mother does,' said the first shoe. 'Mothers are funny – they always love their children even when the children are horrid and rude to them. I should think Jennifer is rude to her mother, wouldn't you?'

Jenny sat down on a form and began to cry. 'I'm *not* rude to my mother, I'm not, I'm not,' she wept. 'I love her. I'm kind to her. Oh, who is it saying these unkind things about me? I may behave horridly sometimes, but I *can* be good when I try!'

'I don't believe that, do you?' said one shoe.

'No,' said the other. 'She couldn't be good! She's one of these spoilt children we've heard about.'

The other children laughed. They were sorry for Jennifer, but they couldn't help thinking that it would do her good to hear these things. She went off crying bitterly, puzzled and unhappy.

The shoes talked all the way. They chatted about

Jenny's bad writing and her wrong sums and her pinching and pushing. Jenny sobbed and cried all the way to the little yellow cottage. The old dame was waiting for her at the gate.

'Dear, dear!' she said, when she saw Jenny coming along with red eyes and tear-stained cheeks. 'What's the matter? Have those shoes been wagging their tongues too much?'

'Shoes? Wagging their tongues?' said Jenny in amazement. 'What do you mean?'

'Well, those shoes I lent you this morning can be most tiresome,' said the old lady. 'They belonged to my great-grandmother, you know, and were made by a brownie, so it is said. They have tongues, of course, just as your own lace shoes have – but these shoe tongues can talk – and talk they do! They are real chatterboxes. I hope they didn't say anything unkind!'

'Oh no, ma'am, we only spoke the truth!' cried the two shoe tongues together, and they flapped themselves about in the shoes. Jenny looked down in amazement.

She took off the shoes very quickly indeed.

'So that's who were speaking!' she said. 'The tongues of my shoes! Well – I never knew shoe tongues could talk!'

'Oh, my dear, they all could at one time,' said the old lady. 'That is why they were called tongues, you know, because they spoke. But they did say the silliest, most tiresome things, so now very few of them are allowed to talk. I can't stop the tongues in this old pair of shoes, though. That's why I called to you to be good this morning – because I knew the shoe tongues would talk about it if you were naughty.'

'I shan't be *quite* so naughty in future,' said Jenny, beginning to smile. 'I don't like to be thought lazy and stupid and horrid. Lend me your shoes in a month's time, and see if they can say heaps of *nice* things about me for a change, will you?'

'Certainly,' said the old lady, slipping Jenny's own shoes on her feet. 'How cross they will be if there is nothing naughty they can chat about!'

THE TALKING SHOES

I'd like to hear what they say in a month's time, wouldn't you? What would *your* shoe tongues say if they could speak, I wonder? Do tell me!

The Inquisitive
Hedgehog

The Inquisitive
Hedgehog

THERE WAS once a most inquisitive hedgehog who liked to know everybody else's business. He used to shuffle round the ditches, listening to all that the toad said to the frog, and trying to find out where the squirrel had hidden his winter nuts.

The pixies that lived in the hedgerow were most annoyed with him, for he was always trying to find out their secrets and, as you know, pixies have many magic secrets that no one but themselves must know. Whenever they met together to talk, they had to be sure to look under the dead leaves or behind the ivy to see if Prickles the hedgehog was hiding there, ready to listen.

Now one day a wizard called Tonks came to visit the pixie Lightfoot, who lived in a small house in the bank of the hedgerow. This house had a little door hung over with a curtain of green moss, so that no one passing by could see it.

Inside the door was a cosy room with little tables, chairs and couches, for Lightfoot often had parties and needed plenty of furniture. There was a small fireplace at one end, and on it Lightfoot boiled his kettle and fried his bacon and eggs for breakfast.

Tonks was to come and have a very important talk with Lightfoot and the other pixies about the party that was to be given in honour of the Fairy Princess's birthday the next winter. Prickles overheard the toad telling the little brown mouse, and he longed to know what day the party was to be, and if the creatures of the hedgerow were to be invited as well as the fairy folk.

But nobody could tell him, for nobody knew.

'Nothing is decided yet,' said the toad. 'And even when it is, I don't suppose we shall know until the invitations are sent out, Prickles. You must just be patient.'

'Yes, but you see, I want to go and visit my grandmother who lives far away on the hillside,' said Prickles. 'And if I choose the week when the party is held, it would be most unfortunate.'

'Well, we shan't miss you very much,' said the toad, going under his stone. He was not fond of the inquisitive hedgehog at all.

Prickles wondered and wondered how he could get to know what the pixies would say when Tonks the wizard came to talk with them. And at last he thought of an idea.

If I creep into Lightfoot's house just before the pixies and the wizard go there to meet, and cover myself with a cloth, I shall look like a sofa or a big stool and no one will notice me. Then I can lie quietly under my cloth and hear everything! he thought to himself. *What a good idea!*

So he borrowed a red shawl from the old brownie woman who lived in the hazel copse, and stuffed it into a hole in the bank where an old wasps' nest had once been. Then he waited impatiently for the evening to come when Tonks was to see the hedgerow pixies.

At last it came. Prickles took his shawl out of the hole and went to where the green moss-curtain hung over Lightfoot's little door. As he crouched there, looking like a brown clod of earth, the door opened and Lightfoot ran out. He was going to fetch some cakes. He left his door open and Prickles quickly went inside. The room was neatly arranged with the chairs and stools in a circle. Prickles pushed them about and made room for himself. He threw the red shawl over his prickly black and crouched down, looking like a couch without a back, or a great stool! He was pleased. Now he would hear everything!

Very soon Lightfoot came back. He was humming a little tune. He put out the cakes neatly on a dish which he placed on a table, and set the kettle on the fire to boil water for some tea.

Presently there was a knocking at the door. Lightfoot opened it. In came the pixies from the hedgerow, chattering and laughing.

'Find seats for yourselves!' said Lightfoot. 'I'm just making the tea. I've some cakes too, if you'd like to help yourselves.'

'We'll wait till old Wizard Tonks comes!' said the pixies. They sat down on the chairs and began to talk. Prickles listened hard with both his ears, hoping to hear a few secrets.

Rat-tat-tat! Someone knocked loudly on the door. It was Tonks the wizard. Lightfoot ran to open it and bowed the old wizard into the cosy room.

'Good evening, everyone,' said Tonks. He was a round, fat wizard, with white hair and a white beard which was so long that he had to keep it tied up in a big knot, or he would have tripped over it.

'Good evening!' cried the pixies, and they all stood

up to greet him, for the wizard was a wise old fellow and everyone respected him.

'Well!' said Tonks, taking off his long black cloak. 'We have come to discuss a most important matter together – the party for the Fairy Princess this winter!'

'Won't you have a nice cup of tea and some cake before you begin the meeting?' asked Lightfoot, coming up with a big cup of steaming hot tea. 'Sit down and make yourself comfortable, Tonks.'

Tonks looked around for a seat. He was fat and rather heavy, so he chose the biggest seat he could see, which, as you have guessed, was Prickles the hedgehog under his red shawl!

Tonks sat down heavily, holding his cup of tea in his right hand and a cake in his left.

But no sooner had he sat down than he shot up again in a fearful hurry, shouting, 'Oh! Oooh! Ow! Pins and needles! What is it? Oooh!'

He was so scared by sitting down on the prickly

hedgehog that he upset his hot tea all over the two pixies that were next to him. His cake flew up into the air and hit Lightfoot on the head when it came down! Dear, dear, what a commotion there was, to be sure!

'What's the matter, what's the matter?' everyone cried.

'Oooh!' said the wizard, rubbing himself hard, for the hedgehog was very, very prickly, and all the prickles had pricked Tonks when he sat down so hard.

'Ooooh!' said the two pixies who had been scalded by the tea.

'Ooooh!' said Lightfoot, wondering what had hit him.

'How dare you put pins and needles on the seat left for me?' roared Tonks suddenly, shaking his fist in Lightfoot's face. 'How dare you, I say?'

'Whatever do you mean?' said Lightfoot, most astonished. 'Don't talk to me like that, please, Tonks. I don't like it. And anyway, what do you mean by throwing your nice hot tea over my friends?'

Prickles began to think he was going to get into trouble. So he very quietly started to move towards the door. But a pixie saw him and shrieked in fright.

'Look at that sofa! It's walking! Oh, look at it! It's gone magic!'

All the pixies looked at what they thought was a sofa, walking towards the door. Tonks looked too.

'Why, that's the sofa I sat down on!' he cried. 'It was as prickly as could be! Catch it! Quick! Catch it!'

Prickles was very frightened. He ran towards the door and just as he reached it, a pixie pulled at the red shawl he had thrown over himself!

'Oh! Look! It's Prickles, the inquisitive hedgehog!' cried Lightfoot angrily. 'He came here and hid himself to hear our secrets. No wonder poor Tonks thought he was sitting on pins and needles! Catch him!'

But Prickles was safely out of the door. He banged it behind him and scurried off through the ditch. He made his way through the stinging nettles, and ran to a hole in the bank that he knew very well. A big stone covered the entrance and a fern grew over the stone. He would hide there!

Tonks, Lightfoot and all the other pixies raced after him. They did not like stinging nettles, so they went round them, and by the time they had got to the other side, Prickles was nowhere to be seen!

'Find him, find him!' raged Tonks. 'I'll teach him to prick me! Yes, I will! I'll pull out all his prickles! 'I'll – I'll – I'll –'

Prickles heard all that Tonks was saying and he trembled in his hole. He was safe there and the stone and fern hid him well. He did hope that no one would find him.

No one did. The pixies hunted for a long time and then gave it up. 'He must have gone to his grandmother on the hillside,' said Lightfoot. 'Let's go back.'

'Now listen!' said Tonks fiercely. 'You keep a lookout for that rascal of a hedgehog all the winter. As soon as he shows his nose, bring him to me! I'll keep a fine meal of cooked needles for him! I'll be going away to Dreamland in the springtime, so find him before then.'

'Yes, Tonks,' said the pixies. 'We are always about this hedgerow, so we shall be sure to see him. Anyway, he will turn up for the party, so we'll catch him then!'

Prickles heard every word, and how he trembled when he heard of the cooked needles! Oh dear!

'I shan't go out of this hole until Tonks has gone to Dreamland!' he decided. 'I'm not going to be caught!'

So, all that winter, Prickles hid in his little hole. He did not go out to catch beetles or slugs, but just curled himself up and slept soundly. He only awoke one night when he heard a great noise of laughing and chattering – and when he poked his nose out, he found that it was the party that was being given in honour of the Fairy Princess's birthday! Poor Prickles! He didn't dare to go to it, and he saw the toad, the frog, the squirrel and the little brown mouse all hopping and running along to have a good time, but he had to keep close in his hole.

It really served him right, didn't it? And do you know, it's a strange thing, but ever since that winter, hedgehogs have always slept all through the cold days! Perhaps they are still afraid of Tonks! I shouldn't be surprised.

The Brownie and
the Witch

The Brownie and
the Witch

ONCE UPON a time Snip the brownie found a yellow toadstool with a blue stalk. He was very pleased, because yellow toadstools with blue stalks have a great deal of magic in them, and Snip thought he could use the magic for making all kinds of spells.

But Deep-One the witch heard of his find, and sent to say she would like to buy it. Snip sent back a note to say that he wasn't going to sell it – and that made Deep-One as angry as could be. So she lay in wait for Snip the brownie, and one day, as he was on his way home from the market in the next town, she jumped out at him from behind a tree.

'Good afternoon, Snip,' she said. 'I want your toadstool.'

'Well, you can't have it,' said Snip, 'because I haven't got it on me! You don't expect me to wear it for a hat or use it for a shoe button, do you? It's at home.'

'Don't be cheeky to *me*,' said Deep-One in a rage. 'I know you've got it at home. I'm coming home with you – and I'm going in at your door – and I'm going to take that toadstool from its hiding place!'

'Oh, you are, are you?' said Snip, thinking as quickly as a rabbit can run.'

Deep-One took hold of the brownie's arm very tightly so that he couldn't run away. Then Snip pretended to be very frightened. He went on through the wood, thinking, thinking, thinking what he could do to save his wonderful yellow toadstool. He came to the end of the wood. He went up the lane and round by the poppy field. He went up the hill – and halfway up he came to a dark little cave running into the hillside.

A curtain of bracken grew around the opening,

and a carpet of moss led to the cave. 'So this is where you live,' said Deep-One. 'Well, I shouldn't choose a dark little cave like this, but I've no doubt *you* like it! Now, whereabouts do you keep that toadstool? You'd better tell me, or you'll be turned into a blackberry on a bush.'

'Please, Deep-One,' said the brownie, 'go right in. You'll find a door at the back. Open it, and take the clock off the mantelpiece. You may find the toadstool behind the clock – if you are lucky!'

The witch went into the cave – but Snip didn't go with her! No – not he! That wasn't where *he* lived! It was the cave of the Ho-Ho Goblin! And the Ho-Ho Goblin didn't like visitors at all – especially those that came in without knocking and took the clock off the mantelpiece!

Snip hid behind a tree to see what would happen – and it wasn't long before he saw quite a lot of things! The witch Deep-One had walked into the cave, opened the door at the back and had gone straight to the little mantelpiece in the room beyond.

She hadn't seen the Ho-Ho Goblin there – but he had seen Deep-One – and with a roar of rage he jumped at her, shouting, 'Thieves! Robbers! Burglars!'

The bad-tempered little goblin caught up his broom and swept the witch off her feet! He swept her out of the door! He swept her out of the cave! Down the hill she went rolling over and over, in the most terrible fright, for she really didn't know what was happening at all.

As for Snip the brownie, he laughed till he cried, and called out to the witch, 'Didn't you find the toadstool behind the clock after all? Well, well, well!'

And after that, Deep-One left Snip alone – he was much too smart for her!

Bubbly's Trick

Bubbly's Trick

BUBBLY WAS a water pixie. He lived in the little stream that ran through Buttercup Meadow, not far from Wizard Twisty's cottage. Bubbly was a mischievous, naughty, tricky little pixie, always having a joke, always playing a prank.

'One day you will get into trouble!' said his brother Trickles. 'It's all very well to play tricks on me, Bubbly, or on the other water pixies – but just be careful not to try your little games on the wizard, or a passing witch!'

'Ooh! That's a fine idea!' said Bubbly at once. 'I'd love to trick old Wizard Twisty. Now let me think!'

'Don't be so silly!' said Trickles and swam off in disgust.

Bubbly sat on a stone under the water and tickled a green frog, and thought and thought. He couldn't think of any trick to play on Wizard Twisty, so he thought he would go up to the cottage where he lived, and see if any joke came into his head there. He swam to the edge of the stream, clambered out among the sweet-smelling water mint and ran through the buttercups and daisies to the wizard's crooked little cottage.

He peeped in at the window. The wizard was stirring a spell in a big dish by the window. He didn't see Bubbly's cheeky face peeping in. The water pixie chuckled and rubbed his hands. He had thought of a fine trick! He would go and buy some sherbet at the sweet shop and when the wizard wasn't looking he would pop it into the bowl of magic – and it would all fizzle up and give old Twisty such a shock!

Off went Bubbly, and bought a pennyworth of

white sherbet at the sweet shop, in a paper bag. He stole back to the cottage and peeped in. The wizard had finished stirring his bowl of magic, and was doing something to the fire at the other end of the room. Now was Bubbly's chance!

In a trice he put his hand in at the window, shook out the powder from the paper bag, and then waited to see what would happen.

The powder fell into the bowl of magic, where strange spells were stirring. As soon as the sherbet touched the magic liquid, there came a great sizzling noise and all the stuff in the bowl rose up like a snowdrift! It frothed over the edges of the bowl on to the table, and Bubbly grinned to see such a sight.

Wizard Twisty turned round when he heard the sizzling noise. He stared at the frothing bowl in the greatest astonishment. Then he rushed to it, shouting, 'The spell has gone wrong! Jumping broomsticks, the spell has gone wrong!'

He took up the bowl and threw all the magic in it

straight out of the window! And, as you know, Bubbly was just outside – so it all went over him in a trice!

He fell down in a fright, soaked through – and oh my, whatever do you think? When he got up, he had turned bright blue! He looked down at himself in horror and fear – a bright blue pixie! Whatever would everyone say to him!

'Oh, oh, oh!' wailed Bubbly, quite forgetting he was just outside the window. The wizard heard him howling and at once popped his head out. When he saw Bubbly there, he growled like an angry dog, stretched out his hand and grabbed hold of the frightened pixie. In a moment Bubbly was standing in the kitchen before the furious wizard.

'Did you put anything into my bowl of magic?' roared Twisty.

'Yes,' sobbed Bubbly. 'I put in some sherbet, and it made it all fizzle up.'

'You wicked, mischievous, interfering, meddling creature!' cried the angry wizard. 'That spell took me four months to make – and now I have thrown it out of the window!'

'It's made me all blue,' sobbed Bubbly.

'Of course it has!' said Twisty. 'It was a spell to make blue lightning – so it turned you blue as quick as lightning! What's your name?'

'B-B-Bubbly!' said the pixie.

'Oho! I've heard of you before!' said Twisty. 'You're the pixie that makes himself a nuisance to everybody by playing stupid tricks. All right – this is the last trick you play! I shall send you to the Gobble-Up Dragon to be eaten!'

Now Bubbly was indeed frightened. He tried hard to think of some way of escape. How could he outwit the wizard? He must think hard!

'Yes!' he said at last. 'Send me to Gobble-Up! I don't care what you do with me so long as you don't drown me!'

'Oh! So you don't mind going to Gobble-Up!' said Twisty. 'Well, if it's no punishment, I won't send you there. I'll pop you into my big saucepan, turn you into a goose, and have you for dinner!'

'Yes, do, do that!' said Bubbly. 'But please, I do beg of you, don't drown me!'

'Oh, so you like being turned into a goose, do you?' said Twisty. 'Well, I'll think of something else. I'll sit you on a broomstick that will take you to the Greeneye Witch. You can be her servant for a hundred years!'

'That would be nice,' said Bubbly. 'Yes, do, do that, Wizard Twisty. Anything, if only you won't drown me!'

'What! You'd like to go to the Greeneye Witch,' said the wizard in surprise. 'Well, I certainly won't send you there! I will turn you into a green frog and give you to my pet duck!'

'Oh, do!' said Bubbly. 'I'd like that – but please – please don't drown me!'

'Well, I think I *will* drown you, seeing that you are so scared of that!' said the wizard spitefully. He caught hold of Bubbly and dragged him out of the cottage and down to the stream. Then he threw him SPLASH into the water, and stood by to watch what happened, rubbing his hands in glee to think what a fearful punishment he had given the pixie.

But Bubbly swam to the other side at once in delight. Then he popped out his cheeky head, now a bright blue, and sang out, 'I'm so pleased to be home, Twisty, I'm so pleased to be home! Many, many thanks to you!'

Then he swam off to tell his brother all about it. The bright blue gradually wore off but he still has blue ears, so if you meet him you are sure to know him. Mischievous, cheeky little Bubbly!

Timothy's Tooth

Timothy's Tooth

ONCE UPON a time a long, long while ago, the fairies were making a spell in a big cauldron over a fire of blue flames. It was a good spell and a wonderful one – a spell to make sick people better. All the pixies and elves bent over the steaming cauldron and watched the colour in it change from red to orange, from orange to yellow, yellow to green, from green to blue – and dear me, then it stopped! Now that was quite wrong, because the enchanted liquid should change through all the colours of the rainbow – it shouldn't stop at blue! It should go on to indigo and then to violet, when the spell would be finished and perfect.

'Ooooooooh!' squealed the elves, in their little high voices. 'We've missed out something!'

'Ooooooooh!' cried the pixies. 'What shall we do?'

Then there was a rush for the big magic book that belonged to the queen, and a great rustle as the thick pages were turned over. A small pixie found the place and read out loud:

'To make the spell perfect, one small white tooth should be added; a child's tooth is best.'

All the little folk looked at one another sadly. 'We shall never get that,' they cried. 'Never! How could we go around pulling out children's teeth?'

'Wait!' said an elf. 'I know a little boy called Timothy, who is very kind. He might give me one of his teeth if I asked him.' So off he flew to Timothy. He told the little boy all about his difficulty and Timothy listened.

Timothy was seven years old. One of his first teeth was very loose indeed. He often waggled it to and fro with his finger, but he wouldn't let his mother take it out, though he knew it wouldn't really hurt. He liked to feel it waggling. But if the elf wanted it to finish the wonderful spell, why certainly Timothy would give him the tooth.

'As soon as my mother comes in, I'll ask her to take out my loose tooth for you,' promised Timothy. The elf gave him a hug. 'Will you put it under your pillow when you go to bed tonight?' he asked. 'I'll come and get it when you're asleep – and for payment you can have a wish that will come true – and perhaps some money too, if I can get some for you!'

Well, Timothy's mother took out the tooth and it didn't hurt a bit. Timothy slipped it under his pillow – and, will you believe it? The next morning the tooth was gone, and a bright shining coin was there instead. Timothy's wish came true, and he was so excited and happy that he told everyone what had happened. The news soon spread, and to this very day, if you put your little white tooth under your pillow, you will find it gone in the morning, and maybe a coin there instead. Don't forget to wish a wish too, will you!

The Enchanted Button

The Enchanted Button

ONCE THERE was a little cheat called Crooky the goblin. He was very clever, so he managed to make a lot of money by his cheating. He kept a little shop and sold nearly everything.

He cheated in nasty little ways. He put in a bad potato or two when Dame Flip called for a basketful. He sold old eggs for new when he could. And he put a few little pebbles into the chicken food that Mother Grumps had from him, for he knew she would never notice the pebbles when she threw the grain to her hens – and certainly the birds wouldn't say anything about them!

Now one day Witch See-a-Lot felt certain that Crooky had cheated her over some fruit. Certainly he weighed it out under her eyes, but he must have taken one or two of the plums out of the bag when he twisted it up.

'I'll give him an enchanted button,' said Witch See-a-Lot with a grin. 'That'll puzzle him a bit – and if he's a cheat, we shall soon know it!'

So the next time that Dame Flap took Crooky's dirty washing home to do, Witch See-a-Lot watched for it to be put on the line to dry. Dame Flap lived next door, so it was quite easy to see it blowing there.

When Witch See-a-Lot saw Crooky's blue shirt drying in the breeze, and knew that Dame Flap had gone out to do her shopping, she grinned to herself. She took up her button box, her needle and cotton and her scissors, and out she went into her garden. She climbed over the wall and jumped down into Dame Flap's yard.

Then she went to where Crooky's blue shirt was

blowing on the line. She snipped off a button, and then sewed on one of her own, which really looked exactly like the one she had taken off. As she sewed she chanted a strange little spell:

'*Button, dear, if Crooky cheats,*
Shout it out to all he meets!
Put him in a dreadful fix,
Make him stop his cheating tricks!'

She snapped off the cotton, and climbed back over the wall, chuckling loudly. Crooky was going to have a fright!

Of course, Dame Flap didn't know anything about it at all. She ironed the shirt and took it back to Crooky the same evening. He put it on clean the next day, and did up all the buttons.

Now, that morning into the shop came Mother Jinks. She wanted a pound of tea. She didn't look at the scales as Crooky weighed out the tea, so he gave her a little less than a pound. But as he was wrapping it up, a little high voice under his chin yelled out loudly, 'Isn't he a cheat? That isn't a pound of tea! *I* watched him weigh it out!'

Crooky almost dropped the parcel in fright. He looked all around to see who had spoken. Mother Jinks stared in astonishment. She was puzzled.

'Put that tea on the scales again,' she said suddenly. So Crooky had to – and, of course, it didn't weigh a pound.

'So you *did* cheat me!' said Mother Jinks in disgust. 'Well, keep your tea! I'll get what I want at the Pixie Stores over the way.' And out she walked.

Crooky was puzzled and frightened. Who had shouted out at him? Who could it have been? He hunted all round the shop and then he heard a little chuckle under his chin: 'I can see you but you can't see me! You're a cheat, that's what you are, Crooky!'

Crooky nearly jumped out of his skin. He felt in

his pockets to see if there was anything magic there, but there wasn't.

'I don't like this,' he said. 'I think I'll just go out delivering potatoes to Father Lucky – and then maybe whatever spell is in the shop this morning will fly away.'

So off he went with his barrow and potatoes. But, of course, he still had on his shirt, and he took that enchanted button with him. It was the top one, just under his chin.

When he got to Father Lucky's, he put a sack of potatoes in the old man's shed. Father Lucky was out so, as there was no one to see him, Crooky put his hand into the sack and took out a few of the biggest potatoes. He knew that Father Lucky would never bother to weigh the sack.

The button didn't say a word. *Ha!* thought Crooky, *I expect the magic was in the shop, then.*

He went back home, and on the way he met Father Lucky. 'I've just taken your sack of potatoes,' said

Crooky to him. 'Finest potatoes I've had. You owe me seven shillings, please.'

'He took out some of the biggest potatoes,' shouted the button. 'He's a cheat. Don't you believe him Father Lucky. Don't you pay him till you get home and weigh that sack.'

Father Lucky stared at Crooky in the greatest astonishment. He couldn't *imagine* where the voice came from!

'I think I *will* weigh that sack before I pay you, Crooky,' he said. 'And if you *have* cheated me, I'll get my potatoes somewhere else. Good morning!'

'Goodness!' said Crooky to himself in dismay. 'This is dreadful really. Where *is* that voice coming from? I've got something enchanted on me, there's no doubt of that. Well, I'll undress myself when I get home and see what it is. Maybe it's an enchanted spider or ladybird.'

So when he got home the goblin carefully undressed himself. He shook out each of his clothes. He emptied his pockets. But he couldn't find a single thing that he thought might be magic. He didn't think of the button, of course! There it sat on the collar of the shirt, a little pearl button that looked exactly like the others!

'Well,' said Crooky, dressing again, 'it's a mystery. I can't find a single thing in my clothes that might be magic.'

As he dressed, he heard the doorbell ring, and in came three customers. Crooky ran into the shop.

'Good morning,' said Mrs Tibble. 'I want six new-laid eggs.'

'Certainly, madam,' said Crooky. He put one old egg into the bag with the five new-laid ones, and handed them to Mrs Tibble.

'Cheat!' said the button. 'One of those eggs is bad! Cheat!'

Crooky was so surprised that he dropped the bag of eggs. They all broke – and a dreadful smell came from one of them!

'What did I tell you?' said the button and it laughed, just under Crooky's chin. 'Pooh! What a smell!'

'I think I'll buy my eggs somewhere else,' said Mrs Tibble in a huff.

'What can I do for *you*, madam?' asked Crooky, very red in the face, to his next customer, who was looking very nervous. It wasn't nice to hear a voice and not see who was speaking.

'I want some apples,' said Miss Wriggle.

Crooky went to get them. He was just about to pop in a bad one, when the button spoke again: 'Now, naughty, naughty, naughty! That's a bad apple and you know it! Cheating again!'

Crooky hurriedly put a good apple into the bag instead. But when he turned round to give them to Miss Wriggle, she had gone – and so had the other customer too. They simply couldn't bear the button's remarks – they sounded too strange for anything.

Witch See-a-Lot popped her head in at the door just then, and grinned.

'Hallo!' she said – to the magic button, not to Crooky.

'Hallo!' said the button at once.

'How are you getting on?' asked the witch.

'Oh, having a fine old time,' answered the button. 'We're cheating hard and I keep talking about it!'

Crooky stared down at his coat and wondered in despair where the voice came from. '*You've* done something magic!' he said to Witch See-a-Lot.

'I have!' grinned the witch. 'But I shan't tell you what! Cheat all you like, Crooky – everyone will know and soon you'll have to shut up shop.'

Well, Crooky didn't cheat at all after that. He really was too much afraid to. Maybe he'll learn one day that it's better to be honest – but if he doesn't, that enchanted button is still on his shirt, waiting to talk. Wouldn't I just love to hear it!

The Seven Crosspatches

The Seven Crosspatches

ONCE UPON a time there were seven crosspatches who caught a little pixie and made him their servant. How hard he had to work for them!

He didn't like the crosspatches one bit because they were just like their name. They were cross old dames, and they made their money by selling spells and magic. They all lived together in a tiny little cottage which had two rooms.

There were seven chairs and a table in one room, and seven small beds in the other. Scurry, the pixie, was kept busy each day making the seven beds and polishing the seven chairs and doing all the cooking for the seven crosspatches.

They were always cross with him and always told him off.

'You're one minute late with our dinner,' one would say to him angrily.

'You've not dusted under my bed properly!' another would say to him.

'You've not wound up the clock!' the third would say. And the others would chime in too, each taking their turn at scolding poor Scurry.

When spring-cleaning time came he was quite tired out. He had to wash all the curtains, all the blankets, all the sheets and all the tablecloths. He had to whitewash the house outside and inside. He had to sweep the two chimneys. The crosspatches kept him hard at work from morning till night.

But he didn't beat the carpets. The magic spells that the old dames were always making made a terrible dust, and because it was magic dust it made Scurry sneeze and sneeze without stopping and gave him the most horrible magic cold.

I'm not going to beat the carpets! he thought. *I shake them every week and that's enough. Let's hope the old crosspatches won't know they've not been beaten.*

But they did know, of course, and they were angry. 'You'll take up each of our seven carpets tomorrow and you'll hang them on the line and beat them!' they said crossly.

'But I shall get a magic cold and sneeze all day long without stopping,' said Scurry. 'And that's very tiring.'

'You can sneeze for a month for all we care!' cried the crosspatches. 'Now, make sure you see to it that every single speck of dust is beaten out of those carpets tomorrow!'

Well, the crosspatches went out the next day because they didn't want to be in the middle of the carpet dust. Scurry took all the carpets and hung them on the line in a row. It made him feel very gloomy.

He began to beat one. His arm soon ached badly. Then an idea came to him. He would pretend he was slapping one of the crosspatches! Everyone wanted to do that, because the seven old dames were mean, bad-tempered and selfish.

He fetched a piece of chalk. He drew one of the crosspatches on a carpet. He put a pointed hat on her head. He laughed, because really he had drawn her very well indeed!

I think I'll draw a crosspatch on each of the carpets! he thought. *Yes, I will. Now this one is the crosspatch that wears a two-pointed hat – and then I'll draw the one that wears a three-pointed hat – then the one with one red rose in her bonnet, and the one with two, and the one with three – and last of all the crosspatch that wears neither hat nor bonnet, but has her hair flying loose!*

So he drew a crosspatch on each carpet. My, they did look funny. Then Scurry took up the carpet beater and began to slap the first crosspatch hard! 'That's for all your bad temper!' he panted, as he slapped a carpet with a drawing of a crosspatch on it. 'That's for all your unkindness!'

Presently two or three of the village pixies came along and looked over the wall at what Scurry was doing.

'Goodness! Wouldn't I like a slap at those horrid old crosspatches!' said one. 'The one with the two-pointed hat that boxed my ears for nothing the other day!'

Scurry was tired and out of breath. He looked round at the pixie and grinned.

'Well,' he panted, 'if you want a good old smack at the second crosspatch, pay me a penny and you can have as many smacks as you like!'

The pixie hopped over the wall at once and paid his penny. Then, with a grin, he took up the carpet beater and hit the carpet hard – the one with the drawing of the crosspatch wearing the two-pointed hat.

'That's for boxing my ears!' he panted. 'And that's for scolding my little sister and frightening her so much!'

'I say! Let me have a turn too!' cried the next pixie,

scrambling over the wall. 'I'd like to beat the last crosspatch, the one who wears her hair loose. She lost her temper with me the other day and stamped all around my garden, trampling on my flowers!'

He paid a penny to Scurry, who was beginning to feel very pleased with himself. He sat well back on the wall, right out of the way of the dust. Soon other pixies came along, and gazed in delight at the two who were slapping away at the carpet on which were chalked the crosspatches everyone disliked so much.

Pennies poured into Scurry's purse. One after another the pixies came and had a good slap at the hated crosspatches. Bang, bang, bang, biff, biff, slap, slap, slap!

'Take that, you horrible, nasty, unkind crosspatch!'

'That's for cheating me out of a whole silver piece the other day!'

'That's for selling me a bad spell that didn't work!'

'That's for making my hens stop their laying!'

All day long the beating went on and soon there was

not a single scrap of dust left in the carpets, not one scrap. It was wonderful.

Scurry's purse was quite full of money. He looked at it. He had never had so much money in his entire life!

When the night came, the pixies went home. They were pleased. They didn't hate the crosspatches quite so much now that they had slapped at them on the carpets. They didn't like hating anyone. It was a nasty, horrible feeling. They all felt much better now!

The seven crosspatches came home and went to bed. Next morning they dragged out the seven carpets to see if Scurry had beaten them well. There was not one speck of dust in any of them! But the thing was that Scurry wasn't sneezing as he usually did when he had beaten the carpets.

'How did you manage to beat the carpets so well?' asked the first crosspatch, the one with the pointed hat.

'I didn't,' said Scurry. 'I got the pixies from the village to beat them for me. They even paid me for letting them beat your carpets!'

'Don't talk nonsense!' said the crosspatch with one red rose in her bonnet. 'Why should the pixies pay you for doing your work for you?'

'Well, you are sure to hear about it, so I suppose I'd better tell you myself,' said Scurry. 'I drew a picture of each of you on the carpets – and the pixies from the village were quite willing to pay me a penny each after that, to beat you on the carpet! They don't like you very much, as you can guess!'

'How dare you! How dare you?' cried all the crosspatches together. 'We'll turn you into a black beetle!'

'You won't!' cried Scurry, running to the door, jingling his money. 'I'm rich now! I'm running away! Goodbye and be careful, crosspatches! It's unlucky to be hated as much as you are. Be careful!'

The crosspatches couldn't catch him, because he ran so fast. They looked carefully at their seven carpets. Yes – they could quite well see the outline of the seven pictures that Scurry had drawn there.

'Dear me!' said the first crosspatch. 'Fancy all the villagers paying to come and beat us on our carpets. Perhaps – perhaps we have been a bit too hard with the pixies. Perhaps we'd better be a little bit more careful now.'

'Yes,' said the second crosspatch, 'because if not they might come to our house and really beat us!'

So they were much nicer after that. As for Scurry, he was so pleased with himself for being able to draw such good pictures that he set himself up as a painter in the woods. In the winter he helps Jack Frost to decorate our windowpanes at night. He does all the funny little twiddly bits. Look out for them, won't you!

Peter Penny

Peter Penny

PETER PENNY the gnome was most tremendously pleased with himself. He had saved up all his money until he had enough to buy a white rabbit to ride on.

So he went to the market and bought one. It was a lovely one, as soft as silk and white as snow. He climbed up on to its back to ride home.

'Off you go!' he cried. And off the rabbit went, lolloping along through the wood. Peter Penny thought it was lovely.

After a little while he met Skippetty Wee, who carried a darling little yellow bird under his arm. Peter Penny got off his rabbit and looked at it.

'What sort of bird is that?' he asked curiously.

'It's a dobbady bird,' said Skippetty. 'She lays an egg for your breakfast and an egg for your tea every day. And fancy, Peter, if you have a friend to tea, she will lay you an extra egg!'

Peter thought it was the most incredible bird he had ever heard of. He wished he had one too.

'Look at my new rabbit,' he said to Skippetty.

Skippetty looked at it. 'All very fine,' he said, 'but it can't lay eggs!'

'No,' said Peter Penny, looking rather upset, 'it can't.'

'Look here,' said Skippetty. 'I know you love eggs. As you're a great friend of mine, I'll change my bird for your rabbit, if you like. Then you'll have eggs to eat every day!'

Peter Penny thought of new-laid eggs every day, and his mouth watered.

'All right,' he said, sliding off the back of his rabbit, 'I'll change over. Give me the dobbady bird.'

So Skippetty gave him the little dobbady bird,

mounted Peter's lovely white rabbit, waved his hand and rode away.

Peter Penny went through the wood, carrying the bird and thinking of new-laid eggs. Presently he met Jinkie the pixie, who stopped and wished him good afternoon.

'Good afternoon,' said Peter. 'Look at my dobbady bird. She lays an egg for breakfast, an egg for tea and an extra one if you have a friend visiting! Fancy that!'

'Goodness!' said Jinkie. 'Fancy eating eggs every single day! How tired you'll get of them, Peter Penny!'

'Oh dear, I hope not,' said Peter Penny anxiously.

'Well, you will,' said Jinkie. 'Look here, and see what *I've* got! This is better than eggs twice every day!'

He put his hand in his pocket and pulled out a little mouse that blinked up at Peter Penny with bright black eyes.

'Oh, it's a dear little mouse!' said Peter Penny. 'But whatever good is a mouse, Jinkie?'

'I'll tell you,' said Jinkie. 'He eats up all the crumbs

that drop down on the floor, Peter, so you don't have to keep on sweeping them up! Isn't that good! It saves such a lot of work, you know.'

Now, Peter Penny was a very untidy eater. He dropped crumbs on to the floor at every meal and was always having to sweep them up afterwards. He thought the little mouse was a splendid idea.

Jinkie guessed what Peter was thinking.

'Listen, Peter Penny,' he said. 'You're a very great friend of mine, so I'll tell you what I'll do. I will give you my mouse in exchange for your dobbady bird. You will never have to sweep up crumbs again!'

'All right,' said Peter Penny, handing Jinkie the little bird. 'I'll swap with you. Give me the little mouse.'

So Jinkie gave him the mouse, took the dobbady bird, waved his hand and went on his way. Peter Penny walked on through the woods with the little mouse in his pocket, thinking how nice it would be not to have to sweep up crumbs any more.

Soon he met Oll the goblin, who was whistling just

like a blackbird on a little silver flute.

'Good afternoon,' said Peter Penny. 'Look at my mouse. He will eat up all the crumbs I drop from my table, so that I don't need to sweep them up. Fancy that!'

'My, my!' said Oll. 'Fancy keeping a tame mouse when you live next door to Witch Wimple and her cat. Why, the cat will sniff it out and eat it in ten minutes!'

'Oh dear! I hadn't thought of that,' said Peter Penny, very worried. 'Whatever shall I do?'

Oll blew a merry tune on his flute. It sounded just like a lark.

'Dear me,' said Peter Penny, 'that's a fine flute! When I first met you it sounded just like a blackbird. Now it sounds exactly like a lark!'

'And now it sounds like a canary!' said Oll, blowing it – and it did. Then he made it sound like a yellowhammer, and then a nightingale, till Peter could hardly believe his ears.

'I wish I'd got a flute instead of a mouse!' he sighed.

Oll laughed. 'Well, as you're a great friend of mine,' he said, 'I'll tell you what I'll do. I'll give you my flute in exchange for your mouse.'

'All right,' said Peter Penny, very pleased. He handed over the mouse. Oll gave him the flute, put the mouse in his pocket, waved his hand and ran off into the woods.

Peter Penny walked on through the wood with the flute hung round his neck, thinking how fine it would be to whistle like a bird.

Soon he met Trippit the elf. She stopped and wished him good afternoon.

'Good afternoon,' said Peter Penny. 'Look at my wonderful flute. It whistles like any bird you care to mention when I blow on it. What do you think of that?'

'Not much!' said Trippit. 'What's the use of whistling like a bird? You just use up all your breath, and it makes you feel quite hungry.'

'Oh dear!' said Peter Penny. 'Does it really? I already

get so hungry I can hardly make my money last. Dear, dear, dear!'

'Just look at what *I've* got!' said Trippit, taking out a little packet. She opened it, and there lay a little steel needle.

'Well, it's only a needle!' said Peter Penny.

'Ah, but listen!' said Trippit. 'It's a wonderful needle. It will mend any hole in your stockings or your clothes all by itself. What do you think of that?'

'Marvellous!' said Peter Penny, thinking of all his torn clothes at home that he never had time to mend. 'Does it really, now? How I wish I had a useful thing like that!'

'Well,' said Trippit the elf. 'I'll tell you what I'll do, Peter Penny. You're a great friend of mine, so if you like, I'll give you my needle in exchange for your whistling flute!'

'Oh, thank you,' cried Peter Penny. He handed over his flute and took the needle. Trippit waved and ran off merrily, playing the flute so that it sounded like a thrush singing after the rain.

Peter Penny went on through the wood, thinking of what a fine time he would have when he set his needle to work, mending all his clothes. He was so busy thinking about it that he didn't look where he was going, and very soon he was lost.

'Oh dear, oh dear,' cried Peter Penny miserably. 'I'm lost – and the night is coming on – and I'm cold and hungry. Oh dear, oh dear!'

He wandered on through the woods for a long time, feeling very tired and cross, but not a house could he see, and not a person did he meet.

At last he sat down on a stone, and cried and cried and cried.

An old witch, riding by on a broomstick, heard him crying, and came down to see what was the matter.

'I'm lost!' said Peter Penny. 'I live on Blowaway Hill and I don't know how to get there. Will you take me home on your broomstick?'

'Oho!' said the witch. 'This needs thinking about.

What will you give me if I do?'

'Can't you be nice and do it for nothing, out of kindness?' asked Peter Penny.

'I'm not a nice person,' said the witch, 'and only nice people do things for nothing. Give me a silver coin and then I will take you home.'

'I haven't any money left,' said Peter Penny. 'I spent it all at the market.'

'What did you buy?' asked the witch.

'A rabbit to ride home on,' answered Peter.

'Well, why didn't you ride home on it?' asked the witch.

'Because I changed it for a dobbady bird that could lay eggs twice a day,' Peter told her.

'Oho! And where's the wonderful bird?' asked the witch, looking all around.

'I changed it for a little mouse that would eat up all the crumbs I dropped,' said Peter sadly.

'Where's the mouse then?' asked the witch.

'I haven't got it,' answered Peter Penny mournfully.

'I changed it for a magic flute.'

'Oho! A magic flute!' said the witch. 'Let me hear you play a tune and then I'll take you home.'

'I haven't got that either,' said Peter, beginning to feel foolish. 'I changed it for a needle that could mend holes by itself! Here it is!'

He showed it to the witch. Her eyes glistened.

'I'll take you home if you give me that,' she told him.

'No!' said Peter. 'I want it.'

'All right,' said the witch, 'I'm going'. And she jumped on to her broomstick.

'Stop! Stop!' cried Peter in panic. 'Don't leave me. I'll give you my magic needle, really I will, if you'll just take me home!'

The witch took his needle and told him to jump on to the broomstick. Then away they went right up into the air as fast as the wind.

Peter Penny held on to the broomstick as tightly as ever he could. He wasn't a bit used to riding on sticks and it felt terribly uncomfortable.

What a horrible way of getting home! he thought. *Why ever didn't I keep my white rabbit, instead of changing it? I could have ridden home very comfortably on that.*

On and on they went, with the wind whistling in Peter Penny's ears and taking his breath away.

Then *phuff*! Off flew his favourite cap into the night and was lost for ever.

Oh my goodness! thought Peter dolefully. *There goes my nice new cap that I bought only last week! But I daren't ask the witch to stop to look for it. She might leave me behind on the ground.*

So he said nothing about his cap, and on and on they went again into the night.

Just as Peter was getting so cold that he thought he really couldn't hold on to the broomstick any longer with his cold hands, he saw Blowaway Hill just below them. The broomstick glided slowly down, and bump! there was Peter at home again.

Before he could say a word, the witch had flown off

again, taking his magic needle safely with her.

Peter Penny was very, very sad. He went into his little house and made himself a nice cup of hot cocoa. Then he undressed and got into bed.

And all night he dreamt of the soft white rabbit he might have ridden on, the dobbady bird who would have laid him mountains of eggs, the little mouse who would have eaten his crumbs, the flute that would have whistled like a bird and the needle that would have mended his clothes.

Then he woke with a jump and cried big tears into his pillow. 'I've been silly,' he wept, 'but I won't be silly any more'.

And you would be glad to hear that he hasn't been silly since then, not even once. So his unhappy adventure brought him some good after all.

The Dog, the Cat
and the Duck

The Dog, the Cat
and the Duck

ONCE UPON a time there lived a little girl called Anna who was taken prisoner by a witch. She lived in the witch's cottage, and did all the work – dusting, sweeping, cooking and mending. Often she tried to run away, but there was a high hedge all round the little garden and search as she might, Anna could never find the way out – only the witch knew that.

'Oh dear, oh dear,' Anna would sigh. 'I suppose I must stay here all my life, working for that horrid old witch!'

Now, with the witch lived a dog, a cat and a duck. The dog used to lie out in the garden all night, guarding the cottage. The cat used to help the old witch with her spells, by standing with her for hours inside a chalk circle which the witch drew on the cottage floor – and the duck used to quack a magic song.

At first the animals took no notice of Anna. They ate the food that she gave them, growled, spat and quacked at each other, and made sure they kept in their own corners.

'Don't you ever speak to them,' the witch warned Anna. 'They are quarrelsome, ill-natured creatures. The cat would scratch, the dog would bite and the duck would peck if you ever tried to make friends with them.'

So Anna left them well alone, until one morning, after a very cold, snowy night, the poor dog crept in shivering from his night watch. He went and lay down by the fire and Anna felt very sorry for him.

Suddenly she had an idea. She waited until the witch had gone out, then she quickly got her little workbasket.

She found some red flannel and began to sew quickly. From time to time she looked at the shivering dog, who lay and growled at the cat whenever she wanted to share the fire.

Anna smiled as she sewed – for she was making a red flannel coat for the dog!

It will keep him lovely and warm at night, she thought. *But, dear me! I don't know how ever I shall get him to let me put it on. I expect he'll try to bite me.*

She sewed on the buttons and at last it was finished. She picked it up and looked at the dog. 'See!' she said gently. 'Here is a nice coat to keep you warm at night. Let me try it on you.'

The dog growled.

'Come!' said Anna, showing him the coat. 'Let me see if it will fit you.'

The dog stopped growling and looked at her. Rather afraid, Anna went over to him and patted his head. He stared at her in surprise. He had never been patted in his life before and he liked it very,

very much. To Anna's immense surprise, he started to speak!

'Do that again!' he said in an odd, husky voice.

She patted him again and he put his great head on her knee. Quickly she slipped the red coat round him and buttoned it. It fitted him perfectly!

The dog twisted and turned himself about to look at it. It felt warm and comfortable. Then he looked at Anna.

'No one has ever been kind to me before,' he said. 'Thank you. Now I shall be warm at night. But do not let the witch see it! I will come to your room morning and night, for you to put the coat on or take it off. Quick! Here comes the witch. Hide it!'

Anna took the coat off quickly, and put it at the bottom of her basket. Then she began mending a hole in her stocking and when the witch came in she didn't notice anything.

Every night the dog came to have his coat put on, and early every morning he slipped through the window of Anna's room to have it taken off. Anna felt happier than she had been, for she knew the dog liked her. She wondered if she could do anything for the cat.

She must get terribly cold feet standing on that stone floor for so long, when the witch makes magic, she thought. *Shall I knit her some little black socks? The witch would never notice them on the cat's black paws.*

She set to work and knitted four funny little black socks. When she had finished them, she took them to the big black cat.

'See,' said Anna kindly. 'Here are some little socks for you to wear when you are standing on the cold floor while the witch makes magic.'

Now the cat had watched Anna being kind to the dog, and had wished she would be kind to her as well. So she purred gratefully, instead of scratching, and let Anna slip on the funny little socks. They fitted perfectly!

'Thank you,' said the cat. 'You are the first person who has been kind to me! These socks will keep my feet nice and warm. Hide them in your room and when I have to help the witch, I will run through and ask you to put them on. She will never see them, for they are just as black as my fur.'

So Anna had another friend, and she smiled to see the cat standing solemnly by the witch every day with a little black sock on each paw!

One day the duck, who had been standing for two hours quacking a magic song for the witch, came to the little girl, and looked at her, and to Anna's great surprise, the bird spoke!

'You have been kind to the dog and good to the cat,' said the duck in a hoarse voice. 'Will you be kind to me too?'

'Why, certainly,' said Anna, very pleased indeed. 'What can I do for you?'

'All that quacking makes my throat very sore,' said the duck. 'Make me a scarf that I can wear round my neck when the witch isn't here.'

'Of course I will,' said Anna, and set to work at

once. She knitted a long, blue, woollen scarf, and the duck liked it very much indeed.

So Anna had three friends, and one day she wondered if they could help her to escape.

That evening, when the witch was out riding her broomstick, Anna sat down by the fire with the dog, the cat and the duck.

'Listen,' she said. 'I want to escape from here. Do you know the way out?'

'I don't,' said the dog.

'I don't,' said the cat.

'And I don't,' said the duck.

Anna sighed.

'But I've got an idea!' said the dog.

'So have I,' said the cat.

'And so have I,' said the duck.

'What?' asked Anna.

'Take the witch's broomstick when she's asleep,' said all three together.

'It will fly over the tall hedge,' said the dog.

'And right up into the sky,' said the cat.

'And away to your home,' said the duck.

So that night Anna stole into the kitchen and took the broomstick from its corner. She opened the door and slipped out with the cat, who was wearing her socks, and the duck, who was wearing her scarf. In the garden was the dog, waiting for her patiently with his red coat on.

'Sit on the broomstick and say:

"*Ringa-maree,*
Listen to me,
Ringa-maray,
Take me away!"'

said the dog.

Anna sat down on the broomstick and looked at her three friends.

'I don't like leaving you,' she said sadly.

'I'll come with you,' said the dog and jumped

on to the broomstick.

'And so will I,' said the cat, and sat down on the broom.

'And so will I,' said the duck, and perched right on the very end of the broomstick.

Then Anna said:

'Ringa-maree,
Listen to me,
Ringa-maray,
Take me away!'

And whizz-whizz-whizz! The broomstick rose in the air and flew right over the tall hedge, taking Anna, the dog, the cat and the duck with it.

All that night they flew, under the moon and the stars, and when the dawn came, the dog gave a growl, the cat a mew and the duck a quack.

'Whatever's the matter?' asked Anna.

'That horrible witch is after us,' said the dog.

Sure enough, far away in the distance was a little black speck running on the ground.

'Take my coat off,' begged the dog. Anna did so and the dog took it and flung it down to the ground far below.

Immediately it grew bigger and bigger, until it lay like a stretch of rough country just in front of the witch. The buttons became big rocks and the four friends watched the witch stop in dismay.

'That will stop her!' chuckled the dog. 'It's a good thing you made me a coat, Anna.'

On they flew, on and on and on. After a short time the three animals all looked downwards once again.

'Quack!' said the duck. 'There she is!'

Anna saw the witch below them. She had climbed over the big rocks and left the stretch of rough country behind. Now she was hurrying after them again to catch them, ready to turn them into beetles, spiders and toads as soon as she came near enough.

'Oh dear!' said Anna. 'What shall we do?'

'Just wait a minute,' said the cat, and pulled off one of her little black socks. She threw it down in the witch's path. Directly it touched the ground, it swelled and swelled and became a great rocky hill up which the witch had to climb.

After a little while the cat drew off another sock and dropped that down too. It swelled into a bigger hill than the first one.

Then the cat flung down her two other socks, and Anna watched them rise up into enormous hills to stop the witch and make her lose her way.

'That will stop her!' chuckled the cat. 'It's a good thing you made me those socks, Anna.'

Anna watched the witch running down the first hill. She came to the second hill, and began slowly climbing up that.

'I really think we're safe now,' said Anna. 'We shall be quite out of sight soon. Hurry up, broomstick!'

On they went again, till suddenly Anna gave a cry of delight – for there below her lay her home, and there was her mother hanging clothes up on the line.

Down went the broomstick to the ground – but just as it reached the grass, the duck quacked loudly in fright. And there was the old witch hurrying towards them, a horrid smile on her ugly face.

'Untie my scarf and throw it at her,' begged the duck.

Anna quickly untied it and flung it at the witch. Immediately it turned into a river of blue, and splash! The witch fell straight into it and was drowned.

So that was the end of her. As for Anna, she ran to her mother and hugged her and hugged her, and told her all that had happened, till her mother could hardly believe her ears.

'And here are my three friends,' said Anna at last, and showed her mother the dog, the cat and the duck.

'They must live with us,' said Anna's mother – and they did. And as the dog guarded them well, and the cat taught them magic spells, and the duck laid them silver eggs every day, you can guess they soon got rich and lived happily ever after.

The Flyaway Brooms

The Flyaway Brooms

PITPAT WAS a very hard-working little gnome. He lived in Dandelion Cottage all by himself, and he made brooms for the fairies. Such lovely little brooms! You would have wanted to buy half a dozen at once if you had seen them.

He made feather brooms, mostly – the sort that have a bunch of feathery plumes stuck on a thin little handle for dusting. The fairies thought they were lovely, and kept Pitpat very busy with orders.

Pitpat was proud of his fine brooms. He thought no one else in the whole of Fairyland could make such beautiful ones, and he boasted of them wherever he went.

Now the Broomstick Witch happened to hear of his boasting one day and she laughed very loudly.

'Silly little boaster!' she said. 'What does *he* know of the art of making brooms? Why, I have been making them for three hundred and sixty-two years, and there are none like mine in the whole kingdom!'

She wrote a letter to Pitpat. This is what she said: 'Dear Pitpat, why do you boast of your brooms? Do you not know that mine are the best that have ever been made? I challenge you to a match, and we will let the fairies choose whose brooms are the best – yours or mine! From the Broomstick Witch.'

When Pitpat got this letter he was terribly upset, and he called all his friends round him to hear it.

'Never mind, Pitpat!' they said. 'Take up her challenge and have a broom-making match. You will win it easily.'

So Pitpat wrote back to the Broomstick Witch, and told her he would certainly have a match with her, and fixed a day in the next week. Then he asked the fairy queen if she would be the judge between them and she said she would.

When the day came there was great excitement. Pitpat went to the market square of Gnome-Town, which was the place chosen for the match. All his gnome friends went with him, besides many elves, fairies and brownies.

The Broomstick Witch arrived in good time. To everyone's surprise she brought nothing with her to make her broomsticks! Pitpat had brought his thin little sticks and a bag of feathery plumes, and thin cord and gum.

'Where is the stuff you are going to make your brooms from?' the onlookers asked the Broomstick Witch in surprise.

'Ha! Ha! Wait and see!' said the witch, grinning broadly.

When the fairy queen came and sat on her silver throne in the marketplace, a bell rang to tell the two rivals to begin.

At once, Pitpat took his little sticks and began deftly binding on his feathery plumes.

The witch clapped her hands and gabbled some magic words. Immediately there appeared her black cat Cinderboy, carrying under his arm a supply of broomsticks and little twigs.

Then the Broomstick Witch set to work. The fairies marvelled to see how quickly her fingers worked, taking up the bendy twigs and tying them firmly and neatly on to the broom handle. As they looked, broom after broom was finished and stood up in a row.

Pitpat worked very fast too. One by one his dear little brooms were finished and laid carefully down in front of him.

When each had made a hundred, the fairy queen came to judge which were the best. Pitpat's hand shook as she looked at his and he longed for her to say he had won.

'Yours are beautiful,' said the queen and took one

up. She dusted her throne lightly with it and thought it very dainty and pretty.

Then she took up one of the witch's brooms and swept the ground with it.

'This is very strong and finely made,' she said. 'I cannot see that there is anything to choose between them.'

'If you please, Your Majesty,' said the witch, 'my brooms are not only for sweeping.'

'What else can they do then?' asked the queen.

'See!' said the witch, and beckoned her black cat to sit on one.

Then, hey presto! The broom rose into the air and away went Cinderboy the cat, with it. When the witch whispered a few magic words, the broom circled gracefully in the air and came to the ground again.

How the fairies stared! As for Pitpat, he couldn't believe his eyes. What an amazing thing for a broom to do!

'Can yours do that?' the queen asked the little gnome.

'No, indeed,' he said sadly.

'Then I am afraid I must say that the Broomstick Witch makes the finest brooms,' said the queen. All the fairies clapped, although they really would much rather that Pitpat had won the match.

Pitpat went home very sorrowful. He kept thinking and thinking about the witch's magic brooms and wishing that he knew the spell that made them fly.

No one will think anything of my brooms now that they have seen those wonderful ones, he thought. *I wish I could get hold of that spell.*

He worried about it so much that at last he picked up his bag and set off for the Broomstick Witch's house.

She lived a long way away and it took Pitpat two days to get there. When he arrived, he saw the Broomstick Witch walking down the road to the town, with her cat Cinderboy.

Pitpat stood and looked after them. Then a naughty thought crept into his mind. He would go and see if he could find that spell in the cottage! Perhaps it would be written in one of the witch's magic books.

So he pushed open the door and went in. The room inside was very small and all round the walls were big magic books. Pitpat took them down one after another and peeped into them.

Then suddenly his heart began to beat, for on the page of one of the books he found a spell to make broomsticks fly in the air! Quickly he got out pencil and paper and copied it down. Just as he finished, he heard footsteps coming up the garden path. He pushed the book back into its place and ran out of the back door just as the witch came in at the front.

When he got home he read his spell again.

'A spell for a broom maker,' he read. 'Those who wish to make brooms that fly as well as sweep should smear their fingers with honey at sunset, and dance by themselves until the moon rises. Then they should dip their fingers into a moonlit pool three times, and let the night moths sup off the honey that is left. When it is all gone and the moths fly away, the spell is in the broom maker's fingers, and whatever brooms he makes will fly like the moths who supped his honey.'

Pitpat excitedly smeared his fingers with honey at sunset, and danced by himself in the woods until the moon rose. He dipped his hands three times into a moonlit pool and then called to the night moths. They came and feasted on the honey still left on his hands. As they supped, Pitpat felt the spell coming into his fingers, and he knew that henceforth he would be able to make brooms that flew!

He told all his friends that he was now as clever as the Broomstick Witch – but he didn't tell them how it was. Everyone was most excited, and begged Pitpat to make flyaway brooms for them.

'I'll make them tomorrow,' said Pitpat, 'and we'll all mount them at once and have our first flight together!'

He made twenty-two for himself and his friends, and most excitedly they all sat on them. Whizz-whirr!

They rose in the air and the fairies and gnomes cried out in delight.

They flew here and there and thoroughly enjoyed themselves for a long time. Then at last they began to feel tired and wanted to go back to earth.

But the brooms wouldn't go! No one knew how to make them fly to earth, and there all the fairies and gnomes were, stranded up in the sky. How frightened and puzzled they felt!

Pitpat was the most frightened of all. He was terribly upset because he knew that he had forgotten to copy down the spell that makes the brooms fly to earth! He knew there was only one thing to be done and that was to fly to the Broomstick Witch and beg her to tell him.

So off he flew, and soon arrived, for the broom went tremendously fast. He hovered above the cottage and called to the witch.

She laughed very loudly when she knew what he had come for.

'That serves you right for copying out my spells without asking my permission!' she said. But she was a good-hearted witch and muttered the words that would take the brooms to earth again.

They all flew to the ground and their riders thankfully tumbled off and ran home. As for Pitpat, he was most unhappy.

'Here. I've got a spell in my fingers that will make brooms that will fly and won't come to earth when they're told to!' he said. 'Now no one will buy my brooms, for everyone will be afraid of them!'

He was right. No one bought his brooms any more. Pitpat was so miserable that he went into his backyard, put all his brooms in a pile and decided to burn them.

Just as he was going to set them alight, all the dandelions that grew round his cottage called out to him.

'Pitpat! Pitpat! Don't burn your flyaway brooms! Give them to us! We will fix them on our seeds, and then they will fly away in the air and find some good place to grow in!'

Pitpat listened in astonishment. What a perfectly splendid idea! Quickly he ran to the dandelions, and, with his gum-brush, gummed a little seed to the handle of his broom, so that the feathery plume stood up straight in the air. Then it flew away all by itself, and the dandelions sighed in delight.

So he didn't stop making brooms. He went on making hundreds and hundreds and gave them all to the dandelions. The flyaway magic in them took them away through the air, and when the magic was all used up the seed fell to earth, and grew up as another dandelion plant.

And Pitpat was as happy as could be, and never stole a spell again in his life. You can easily see what dear little brooms he makes if you look – for every dandelion seed has one to help it to fly away to this very day!

Acknowledgements

All efforts have been made to seek necessary permissions.

The stories in this publication first appeared in the following publications:

'The Goblin's Dog' first appeared in *Sunny Stories*, No. 5, 1937

'The Most Peculiar Knocker' first appeared in *Sunny Stories*, No. 374, 1946

'The Bonfire Folk' first appeared as 'The Bonfire-Folk' in *Sunny Stories*, No. 152, 1939

'Tell-Tale!' first appeared in *Enid Blyton's Magazine*, No. 11 Vol. 2, 1954

'A Peculiar Adventure' first appeared in *Sunny Stories*, No. 444, 1948

'The Wishing Jug' first appeared in *Sunny Stories for Little Folks*, No. 133, 1932

'The Moon in the Pail' first appeared as 'Chapter 16' in *Bimbo and Topsy*, 1943

'The Enchanted Shoes' first appeared as 'The Enchanted Slippers' in *Sunny Stories for Little Folks*, No. 191, 1934.

'The Little Brownie House' first appeared in *Sunny Stories*, No. 191, 1940

'The Wizard's Needle' first appeared in *Sunny Stories for Little Folks*, No. 101, 1930

'The Blackberry Gnome' first appeared in *Sunny Stories for Little Folks*, No. 80, 1929

'The Whispering Pool' first appeared in *Sunny Stories*, No. 341, 1944

'Millicent Mary's Surprise' first appeared in *Sunny Stories*, No. 212, 1941

'A Strange Thing to Happen' first appeared in *Sunny Stories*, No. 535, 1952

'Twinkle Gets Into Mischief' first appeared in *Sunny Stories for Little Folks*, No. 211, 1935

'The Fairy in the Cracker' first appeared in *Sunny Stories*, No. 553, 1953

'The Storm Fairies Get Into Mischief' first appeared in *The Teachers World*, No. 1167, 1926

'Fiddle-De-Dee's Spell' first appeared in *Sunny Stories for Little Folks*, No. 232, 1936

'Peronel's Magic Polish' first appeared as 'Peronel's Polish' in *The Teacher's Treasury*, Vol. 1, 1926

'The Wrong Side of the Bed' first appeared in *The Teachers World*, No. 1637, 1934

'The Talking Shoes' first appeared in *Sunny Stories*, No. 226, 1941

'The Inquisitive Hedgehog' first appeared in *Sunny Stories*, No. 4, 1937

'The Brownie and the Witch' first appeared in *The Teachers World*, No. 1784, 1937

'Bubbly's Trick' first appeared in *Sunny Stories for Little Folks*, No. 244, 1936

'Timothy's Tooth' first appeared in *The Teachers World*, No. 1645, 1934

'The Enchanted Button' first appeared in *Sunny Stories*, No. 148, 1939

'The Seven Crosspatches' first appeared in *Sunny Stories*, No. 368, 1945

'Peter Penny' first appeared in *The Teacher's Treasury*, Vol. 1, 1926

'The Dog, the Cat and the Duck' first appeared in *The Teacher's Treasury*, Vol. 1, 1926

'The Flyaway Brooms' first appeared in *The Teachers World*, No. 1180, 1926

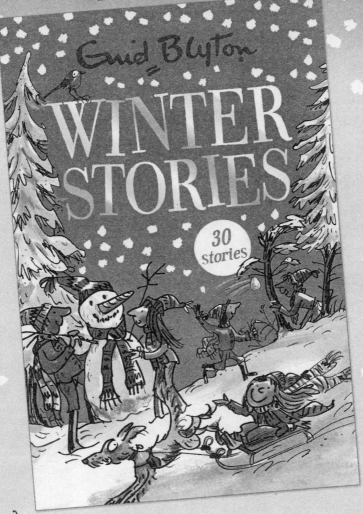

THE SECRET SEVEN

READ ALL 15 CLASSIC STORIES!

THE SECRET SEVEN

SOLVE THE MYSTERY!

And don't miss…

The Secret Seven are back in a brand-new mystery by
prizewinning author Pamela Butchart!

Enid Blyton

is one of the most popular children's authors of all time. Her books have sold over 500 million copies and have been translated into other languages more often than any other children's author.

Enid Blyton adored writing for children. She wrote over 600 books and hundreds of short stories. *The Famous Five* books, now 75 years old, are her most popular. She is also the author of other favourites including *The Secret Seven*, *The Magic Faraway Tree*, *Malory Towers* and *Noddy*.

Born in London in 1897, Enid lived much of her life in Buckinghamshire and adored dogs, gardening and the countryside. She was very knowledgeable about trees,

flowers, birds and animals. Dorset – where some of the Famous Five's adventures are set – was a favourite place of hers too.

Enid Blyton's stories are read and loved by millions of children (and grown-ups) all over the world. Visit enidblyton.co.uk to discover more.